"You loo___
sleep."

"I was feeling very sexy," Jilly murmured. She'd been having a dream in which she and Kit had great sex on the front seat of the Jaguar. In dreams, impediments like stick shifts, and the curious eyes of other drivers didn't exist. Their coupling had been graceful and easy and hot. "Actually," she added, "I still feel pretty sexy."

Kit leaned over to touch her knee. "Luckily, it's not that far to Key West," he teased.

"Yeah." Jilly straightened in her seat, pulling her dress down over her knees. She smiled briefly, but secretly his sensible reaction depressed her.

Grow up, Sanderson, she thought. *The fact that you've discovered the joy of sex so recently doesn't mean that he has.* What had she expected? That he would reach under the hem of her sundress and caress her bare thigh? Lean over at the next stoplight and kiss her passionately? Be so overcome with desire that he would pull into the nearest motel?

A minute later, Kit brought the car to a swift halt in front of the "Island Motor Court" sign. Giving her a swift, hard kiss, he said, "C'mon, Jilly. Let's take a walk on the wild side."

Suzanne Scott, a professional writer for more than fifteen years, came up with the idea for *One Hot Summer* when she first decided to spend part of the year in Florida. The blue skies and sandy beaches were a big change from her hometown, New York City! After visiting Key West, then Miami, she couldn't help being struck by the contrast between the two places. One was so funky, laid-back and eccentric, the other so fast-paced and cosmopolitan. She immediately began playing the writers' game of "what if?" and her first novel was born.

ONE HOT SUMMER
Suzanne Scott

Harlequin Books

TORONTO • NEW YORK • LONDON
AMSTERDAM • PARIS • SYDNEY • HAMBURG
STOCKHOLM • ATHENS • TOKYO • MILAN
MADRID • WARSAW • BUDAPEST • AUCKLAND

For Victoria Donnelly,
my sister and friend.

ISBN 0-373-25747-3

ONE HOT SUMMER

Prologue

IT WAS A BALMY APRIL Sunday and Truelove House looked its faded old-fashioned best. Worn white lace curtains hung from its shuttered windows and rustled gently in the Key West breeze. A handful of guests strolled lazily along the paths of the overgrown garden, breathing in the exotic scents of mimosa and hibiscus. The gold-lettered sign swinging near the whitewashed gate provided the only hint that the place was a bed-and-breakfast inn rather than a private home.

Lavinia Malone sat on her shady porch and surveyed the inn. It was all very charming, she acknowledged. Orderly. Well organized. But it was dull, dull, dull.

What was lacking was surprise, she decided. Truelove House was less exciting than support hose and more predictable than toast. It was her own inn, and it still bored her silly. It was a sad state of affairs. Even at a frail and fading ninety, Lavinia Malone hated being bored.

Truelove House hadn't always been so sedate. When she and Sam had first bought the place as newlyweds over sixty years ago, they'd been so dizzy with infatuation for each other they could barely sign the contracts. Laughing, they'd made love on each of the thirteen guest beds and named the inn in honor of their vows to each other. The rooms had echoed with their tempestuous romance and the equally colorful dramas of their children, staff and guests. Back then Truelove House had been a place of energy, conflict and passion.

But then Sam had died, and Lavinia herself had grown older. These days, Truelove House was a well-run business. A pleasant haven for visitors savoring the eccentric charm of the Florida Keys. A good investment. Not that Lavinia needed the income. Sam had left her well provided for, and she had a very successful, very generous grandson.

These days, the inn's plumbing worked and the porters managed to find the right rooms and even the visitors were staid people, respectable and well behaved. Long married couples. Sensible families. Single executives.

Even at ninety, Lavinia Malone didn't care much for staid, respectable people.

Lavinia had no regrets at all, no sense of having left anything undone. Her one final desire, she thought, rocking energetically in her chair, was for this beloved place to be filled with excitement once more. That would be her last wish, her monument, her legacy. She was too old and too tired to make it happen herself, but suddenly she fiercely wanted it done.

The only question was how.

Lavinia's gaze wandered to the inn's garden as she thought. A half hour later, she'd hit upon the perfect plan. She pushed herself up out of her chair and made her way carefully inside. She would tell Benjamin Knowles, her lawyer, to make the necessary changes in her will. He wouldn't like this idea. It would offend his cautious legal mind, but she didn't care. Her plan would rejuvenate the inn, draw in new guests and give a few local people work. And maybe even jolt two of the people she loved most out of their ridiculous mule-headed ideas about who they were and what they needed from life.

Lavinia picked up the telephone, her clear gray eyes gleaming with mischief. Yes, whatever happened, her plan would shake them up a little.

And both of them, in her decided opinion, needed shaking up very much indeed.

1

JILLIAN SANDERSON STOOD in the middle of her antique shop and scowled.

All of her stock was polished and enticingly arranged. All of the fancy labels that were one of the shop's trademarks were written and tied to their items with tiny bows. A neat row of custom gift baskets stood by the door awaiting delivery. On her desk, folders for each of her current interior-decoration projects were organized and up-to-date. She'd even had time to put out a plate of biscuits and a vase of bright pink tulips.

She loved her shop. Business was booming. She was...bored.

You are not bored, a voice in her head scolded.

"I am too," she said aloud.

You came here to relax. You decided you wanted to open an antique shop because it was soothing. You chose Key West because it was lazy and tolerant and undemanding, the voice insisted.

"You can't relax forever. Antiques are fine. Key West is fine," she said, refolding an embroidered shawl. "It's my own life I can't stand."

Okay, then, said the voice. *So, just what is it that you want?*

"A little...excitement?" she asked herself dubiously.

Great. This was getting her nowhere. Kneeling down near the sales desk, she dragged out a cardboard box filled with old tea things she'd just bought at auction. The sterling trays, pitchers and creamers hadn't been polished in a hundred years.

There was nothing like polishing old tarnished silver to use up a woman's excess energy in a productive way.

She twisted the lid of the silver polish open and had another thought. Putting two fingers in her mouth, she whistled softly.

A furry brown head emerged from a pile of needlepoint cushions. A pair of wide yellow-green eyes gazed at her calmly. Pankhurst was no stranger to being consulted.

"Pankhurst," Jilly said to her cat as though reciting a magic spell, "make something happen." She paused. That didn't sound right. "Make something exciting happen." She stopped again. The cat looked encouraging. "Make it happen now."

"Jilly," said an amused voice from the doorway, "I have two pieces of news for you. The tooth fairy has retired to San Diego and taken up cactus gardening, and if you want excitement you have to talk to somebody other than a cat."

"Margaret." Jilly blushed. "I was just...making conversation."

"Of course. I'm sure it drives the cat crazy when you don't keep up your end."

"Very funny. Actually, you should have come in a few seconds earlier. Back then I was talking to myself."

Margaret grinned as she walked toward the sales desk. Her wooden earrings clinked, her silver bangles tinkled, the beads at the end of her short brown cornrows drummed and her batik caftan rustled around her. Margaret Greer, Jilly thought fondly, was a walking one-woman symphony. "Here, have a doughnut," Margaret said. "Loaded with fat. It will clog your arteries in sixty seconds. That's enough excitement for ten o'clock in the morning on a July Tuesday."

"Yeah. Arteriosclerosis. Every woman's festive summer fantasy," Jilly said. "Come and sit down."

"So. I'm curious. Exactly what kind of excitement was it that you were asking your cat for?" Margaret settled her ample form into the chair next to Jilly's desk. She was Bahamian, descended from some of the Key's original settlers—in island lingo, a true Conch. At fifty, she'd managed Truelove House for twenty years. She was wise and sassy and a terrific friend.

"I'm not exactly sure," Jilly answered. "That's the problem."

"It's the off-season. Maybe you just need to get away. You could go shopping in New York or canoeing in the Loire Valley or mountain climbing in Colorado," Margaret said.

"No. I may not be sure what I want, but what I definitely don't want is the kind of excitement you have to decide on and plan and pay for." Jilly fished a doughnut from the bag. "Can I have this French cruller? I want...the kind of excitement that's a total surprise. That transforms your life in an instant. That you'd never think of in a million years. Like when the elf with the three wishes shows up in a fairy tale."

Margaret smiled. "It could happen."

Jilly shook her head. "It would probably be better if it didn't. The last time anything truly unexpected happened to me was in seventh grade, when Billy McIntyre, the cutest guy in the class, asked me to dance at the Peachtree High junior prom. I was dumbfounded, and so was everyone else. It was about as likely as Bob Dole putting his hand up Sandra Day O'Connor's skirt. "

"What happened?"

"We started to do the Latin hustle and he threw up all over me," Jilly said. "Too much pink punch, I guess. I never lived it down. It was the beginning of my long history of adoring really terrible men. God, this is depressing. Let's change the subject. How's Truelove House?"

"Lousy," Margaret sighed. "Well, business is fine, at least for this slow time of year. But I miss that darned Lavinia Malone something fierce. The funeral was only six days ago, but it seems like I've been rattling around the inn by myself for a hundred years."

"I can imagine," Jilly said, handing her the bag of doughnuts. "Here, have another. I miss her terribly, too, and I have distractions. I'm not spending all my time in her hotel. It must remind you of her constantly."

"Well, you loved her. So did I. Actually the memories cheer me up sometimes. I was checking the monthly accounts yesterday and I could have sworn I heard her yelling at me to stop being such a boring bean counter and come enjoy the sunshine." Margaret grinned.

"That sounds exactly like her. What did you do?"

"I finished the accounts, of course. That's why I'm a boring bean counter. Anyway," Margaret said, waving a walnut-colored arm, "I don't need the tan."

Jilly licked some excess glaze from her fingers. "What's going to happen with the inn?"

"Lavinia's will stipulated that I'd keep my job, so I don't have to worry. There will be some changes, though. Lavinia's grandson is down here meeting with her lawyer right now."

Jilly made a face. "You mean the hotshot moneyman who didn't make it to her funeral?"

"That's the one. Don't be so judgmental, child. He's a busy man with a complicated job," Margaret said, fishing the last pastry from the bag. "Want to split this? I have my figure to consider."

Jilly smiled as she reached for her half. Margaret's figure had been large and majestic for years. "He's a jerk."

"You've never even met him."

"He's still a jerk. Plenty of people I haven't met are." *Not to mention the ones I have. Met. Married. Whatever.*

"Christopher has his strengths and his weaknesses, like all of us," Margaret said, wiping off her sugary hands on a paper napkin. "Lavinia loved him very much."

"True. I'm willing to give him a few points for that. He definitely made her happy. But you know as well as I do how much she loved Sam, and according to Lavinia, her beloved Christopher is Sam's spitting image. I think she kind of got the two confused." Jilly crumpled the brown paper doughnut bag and tossed it into her chintz-covered garbage can.

"You know," she added, squinting consideringly at her friend, "you have this annoying Mona Lisa, Delphic oracle, cat-in-the-cream-bowl look that tells me you know something I don't."

"You're right. I do," Margaret said smugly.

"About what?" Jilly was suspicious. "About the great Kit Malone? About the Truelove Inn? About my chances for some excitement in the next century? What?"

Margaret shook her head. "I'm sorry it came up. I'm not saying another word right now, Jilly. You'll hear about it soon enough. I'm going to be discreet."

"Oh, is that what you're being? I thought you were just being irritating," Jilly said.

"I brought you doughnuts and gave you a chance to talk with someone who could actually form words. Be grateful for that." Margaret lifted herself from her chair, smoothed her caftan over her hips, and headed for the door.

"Oh. And about needing some excitement," she added

over her shoulder. Jilly looked at her inquiringly. "Don't worry. I'm sure something will turn up."

"I know it will. For better or for worse," Jilly said, holding open the shop door.

"How in the world do you know that?"

Jilly grinned. "Pankhurst never lets me down."

"SHE WHAT?" KIT MALONE'S voice rose. The front legs of the antique Windsor chair in which he had been elegantly but precariously balancing hit the Oriental rug with a thud. "Say that again."

Benjamin Knowles looked forbiddingly at his visitor. Clients of Benton, Benton & Knowles rarely raised their voices and never, but never balanced on the back legs of their chairs. The fact that Kit was an old family friend and the grandson of one of Ben Knowles's oldest clients gave him a certain amount of leeway. So did the fact that the lawyer had always secretly enjoyed the younger man's ferocious intensity. Even at a supposedly mature thirty-seven, even sitting in the dim hush of a lawyer's office on a lazy summer morning, even wearing a conservative navy suit, Kit Malone exuded enough energy to produce unassisted fission. He wasn't a person, Ben thought. He was a force of nature.

However, Benton, Benton & Knowles had its standards. Even for Kit Malone.

"Certainly, Christopher," Ben said. The lawyers of Benton, Benton & Knowles never used nicknames in business hours, either. "Let me repeat in more detail.

"As you know, your grandmother left her estate to you as her closest surviving relation. She also made several special bequests. Specifically, she has left a 50 percent share of her inn, Truelove House, to a local decorator and antiques dealer, a Jillian Mabel Sanderson. You and Ms.

Sanderson will act as co-owners of the business and share equally in any profits it may generate."

The attorney paused. "Do you follow?"

A dog could grasp it, Kit thought. "Go on, Ben," he said, folding his arms over his chest and rebalancing himself on the back legs of his chair.

Fussily Ben turned over one of the onionskin pages on his desk. "This bequest is subject to one condition. Mrs. Malone requested that Ms. Sanderson and yourself redecorate the inn, using capital she has put in trust. The redecoration must be completed by the sixty-fifth anniversary of Mrs. Malone's wedding to your grandfather Samuel, which is November 12 of this year. Otherwise, Mrs. Malone directs that Truelove House be sold and the proceeds divided between you. The details are explained in the will, which I have for you here," Ben concluded.

"I've heard it twice, but I still don't believe it." Kit closed his eyes briefly, gritting his back teeth. "Then again, why am I surprised? This is the woman who gave me a goat for my thirteenth birthday. This is the woman who was disappointed when I got into Yale because she wanted me to go to college someplace really interesting, like Peru. This is the woman who ran for mayor on the platform that Key West should secede from the Union and nearly won. I should have known something was up. Even for a sick ninety-year-old lady, she was acting too damned docile." He scowled. "If she wasn't already gone, I'd kill her."

Ben Knowles looked scandalized. "Christopher. Really. Your grandmother just passed away. That is not a very...seemly remark."

"We didn't have a very seemly relationship. We loved each other, but that's a different thing." A half smile twitched the corner of Kit's mouth. "We told each other the truth, about which we rarely agreed, and we let the chips fall where they would."

"The truth here, Christopher," Ben said sternly, "is that this admittedly odd arrangement does you no financial harm. The sum set aside for the redecoration is ample, and the rest of the estate is large enough to make Ms. Sanderson's bequest unimportant."

"The truth, Ben," Kit retorted, "is that I could have afforded to refurbish the Waldorf-Astoria if Lavinia wanted me to. I have plenty of money. I don't have plenty of time. I could cope with inconvenience. But this... It's impractical. Romantic. Probably impossible." He glared at the lawyer. "Frankly, I can't believe the two of you did this to me," he said.

Sighing, Ben relented. "I did try to suggest to your grandmother that the bequest was perhaps a touch too...imaginative."

"What did she say?"

Ben frowned.

"Come on, Ben. Trust me. Attorney-client privilege does not apply," Kit said. "Spit it out. You owe me."

"She called me—how exactly did she put it?—a fuddy-duddy old fusspot," Ben said. "It did not amuse me, Christopher. Do not laugh."

Kit laughed. *Works for me, pal.* "Sorry, Ben. If it makes you feel any better, she's called me far worse. It was her way of showing affection. False politeness bored her to tears."

"I, personally, would have preferred it. In any case, however, she was entitled to do as she pleased," Ben said stuffily, returning to the documents in front of him.

Kit raked a hand through his hair. "Yeah. Well, my clients are entitled to insist that I do the job they pay me for. Which means sitting in Miami watching their stock portfolios, not wandering around Key West choosing curtains."

"If you and Ms. Sanderson simply ignore the renovation and allow the November 12 deadline to pass, you can force the inn to be sold," Ben said craftily.

"No." Fiercely Kit shook his head. "Absolutely not. Lavinia was the only family I had. That crazy hotel was her life. If she wanted it redecorated by this Sanderson dame, this Sanderson dame is damned well going to redecorate it. Even if I have to stand over her with a whip."

"I'm sure that won't be necessary," Ben replied.

"Too bad," Kit said. "I'm feeling aggressive, and I wouldn't mind taking it out on somebody. Even a little old lady."

Kit stood and prowled restlessly toward Ben's glass-fronted bookcases, staring unseeingly at the rows of leather-bound books inside them.

Damn it, Lavinia, he thought. Kit could picture this Jillian Sanderson perfectly. Even her name was old-fashioned. No one had named babies Mabel in fifty years. She'd be old, elegant, tough, opinionated and wildly eccentric, he'd bet, just like his grandmother. And like Lavinia, probably stubborn as hell.

Ben Knowles neatened his desk carefully, avoiding Kit's eye. "What makes you think that Ms. Sanderson is old?"

Kit cocked one eyebrow and stuck his hands on his hips, staring down at Ben. "Why? Have you met her? Do you know something you're not telling me?"

"Really, Christopher. I have not had the pleasure of meeting Ms. Sanderson. Your grandmother assured me that she is a person of character and integrity, and she is well respected locally," Ben said primly.

Sure, Kit thought. *Probably wins good-conduct prizes at the Key West bingo league.*

Silently he chided himself for .the mean-spirited thought. If only he didn't have this irrational hatred of resort towns. And a business partner who was probably suffering from apoplexy back in Miami. If only he wasn't waiting to find out about a new account that they desperately wanted. If only he didn't have several million dollars riding on a stock market that he didn't have time to watch.

"Christopher?" Ben prompted.

"What? Sorry. Oh...the Sanderson woman. Well, I can't imagine that she's as old as Lavinia, but it's logical to bet that she's—mature. I assume that this was one of Lavinia's ploys to help one of her impoverished friends. Widows, well-meaning couples on Social Security, aging gentlewomen living on a shoestring—you know how she was. I can't imagine any other reason why else she'd cook up a scheme like this."

"Well, I'll be glad to make an appointment in order to notify Ms. Sanderson, then," Ben said.

"That won't be necessary, Ben." Kit resigned himself to the inevitable. He hadn't made a fortune on Wall Street by denying unpleasant realities. Truelove House and Ms. Jillian Mabel Sanderson were not about to go away just because he wasn't in the mood for interior decoration.

He glanced at his thin gold watch. It wasn't even ten yet. He could wrap things up in Key West and still be back in Miami by the time the market closed at four. An hour or so to get to and from the shop, an hour to conduct a little research and an hour to convey the news and his wishes to his grandmother's friend—politely but in no uncertain terms.

We may be co-owners, Kit thought, *but I'm going to hold the reins.*

"I'll be happy to tell Ms. Sanderson the news, Ben," he said smoothly, "if you'll give me a copy of the will. I'll have her call you about the paperwork. And I'll be in touch myself, of course."

Kit shook Ben's hand, picked up his briefcase and strode toward the double doors opening onto the reception area. With his hand on the brass doorknob, he stopped short.

Something stunk here, damn it.

"Ben?" he said impulsively. "Lavinia never did anything without a reason, and you don't seem convinced the reason for this dim-witted scheme was to help a friend. So tell me. Just what do you think she had in mind when she cooked it up?"

The lawyer's eyes gleamed with what might have been amusement. But he remained discreetly noncommittal to the end.

"Your grandmother did not explain her thoughts to me, Christopher, and it is not for me to speculate," he answered. He permitted himself a hint of a smile. "All I can say," he finished, opening the heavy door and waving Kit through it, "is that I wish you the very best of luck in finding out."

A FEW HOURS LATER, the hot island sun had reached its daily peak. Laughing groups of people ambled among Old Town's hibiscus trees and restaurant courtyards, seeking cold drinks and shade. The tourists wore sunglasses, garish T-shirts, baggy shorts and sunburns. The locals, as far as Kit could tell, wore suntans and rags.

Kit Malone hated resort towns. Key West might have been his beloved grandmother's home, but it was no exception. He hated the air of lazy relaxation, the cheerful tackiness of the souvenir shops, the clusters of chattering tourists, even the seductively gentle breeze. He strode grimly down Whitehead Street, determined to get in and out of this perfectly charming madhouse as soon as hu-

manly possible. Once the matter of Ms. Jillian Mabel Sanderson was settled to his satisfaction, he'd be heading out
of the Keys just as fast as his beloved 1966 Jaguar X-model
could take him.

Do-nothings, Kit thought impatiently as he shouldered
his way through the clusters of sightseers. Losers. Drifters.
Kit had been one of those people once. For a single year
more than a decade ago, clear across the continent. He'd
lazed in the sun and gone with the flow. In the end he'd re-
gretted it, badly. Since then he'd avoided resorts. He
stayed in Miami, where he belonged. Where men wore
suits, where women had manicures, where everyone
seemed to have someplace to go and something to do.

Striding along the narrow sidewalks, Kit cursed his sudden decision to walk to Jillian Sanderson's shop. His suit
clung to his legs and his discreetly striped Sea Island cotton shirt stuck to his back. He felt messy and out of place.
He never felt out of place. The feeling ticked him off. *I don't
know where you are, Lavinia,* he thought, *but I hope you appreciate this.* A bead of sweat trickled down his jawline. *And I
hope you have air-conditioning. One of us should be comfortable.*

Olivia Street. *Finally,* Kit thought. He turned off Duval
Street and scanned the street numbers impatiently. He ap-
proached the right storefront from an angle, determined
not to be seen until he'd fully checked the place out. It
would be nice to have some advance idea of exactly what
Lavinia had gotten him into.

Jillian Sanderson's shop wasn't sedate, cluttered or
dark, the way Kit had imagined it. The shop awning with
its italic *JILLY'S* was a cheerful blue, green and yellow
stripe. Stone urns cascading with pink ixora, glossy ivy
and sky blue plumbago stood on either side of the small-
paned door. In the display window an old wooden Hoo-
sier cabinet was filled with colorful kitchenware. A pair of

old wooden chairs stood on a rag rug beside it. Kit snorted to himself. *In Key West this might be antiques,* he thought. *But in Miami, it's junk.*

He pushed open the door and walked into the shop's cool interior.

THE BELL OVER THE shop door tinkled loudly. Jilly Sanderson looked up from her desk. She was on the phone, but she gave the customer who entered a quick appraising once-over. A man, which was unusual. A confident, purposeful and irritated man, which was even stranger. Jilly made an impish face at his extremely well-built back. *Go ahead, gorgeous,* she thought. *Pretend you run the world.*

At least he seemed happy on his own. She turned her attention back to the phone, on which Maisie DuMaurier was dithering. Like many decorating clients, Maisie had trouble making up her mind. "No, Maisie," Jilly said patiently, rubbing at the handle of a stubbornly tarnished old pitcher as she listened. "I don't think an Oriental print would be better than the cabbage rose chintz. The chintz looks great with the stripe you chose for the powder room. No, blue wouldn't be an improvement. That soft dusty pink is just what you want in a bedroom. Besides, Maisie, everything's been ordered, so we have nothing to lose by at least seeing it," Jilly coaxed, glancing to make sure that her customer was still occupied.

He was. He circled her tiny, crowded shop like a lion surveying a rather inadequate lair. He was much too large, too intense, too powerfully male for the space, and also too arrogant to know it. Not to mention sexy, Jilly thought. Unruly black hair. Shrewd but beautiful ice gray eyes. Sensitive mouth, quirked up at one side with impatience. Obnoxious, but probably great in bed.

Whoa, girl, Jilly thought, surprised.

She gave herself a fierce mental shake. What in the world was she thinking of? She never mixed business with pleasure. She rarely had that kind of pleasure, period. More to the point, she hated suave well-tailored city types. Her divorce from the extremely suave and well-tailored F. Claude Henderson—not to mention the four years of marriage that preceded it—had left enough scars for a lifetime.

Besides, it wasn't as though a man like the one prowling through her shop would choose a woman like Jilly Sanderson, anyway. He'd want a curvaceous blonde. Or a brunette with impeccable Social Register standing. Or one of each. Not a freckled thirty-two-year-old ex-tomboy with no figure to speak of and—Jilly peered down—silver polish under her fingernails. Even Claude had only married her for the challenge of making her into his fantasy of a society wife. It hadn't worked. If Jilly ever dated anybody seriously again, which she doubted, it certainly wasn't going to be some arrogant goon in a Brooks Brothers tie.

Still, she wished she was wearing something better than her usual summer Tuesday sundress. Or at least that her hands were clean.

Kit listened to her talk about color schemes with half an ear while he finished his survey of the shop. None of the merchandise fit his taste, which ran to the sleek and ultramodern. Grudgingly, though, he had to concede that it all looked prosperous and well organized. This was no ditsy amateur operation. Appealing, he decided. Not chic, not serious, not truly impressive. But definitely appealing, in a goofy kind of way.

For the first time, Kit turned his attention to the woman behind the glowing oak sales desk. Too bad this wasn't the boss, he thought. She was as appealing as the shop, in the same quirky way. Not his type, definitely. Not classically beautiful enough. Not drop-dead sexy enough. And too...vulnerable looking. But cute, very cute. She was thirty or so, he guessed. She had gleaming light brown hair cut in a boyish cap, which tumbled casually onto her forehead in front but was short enough in the back to reveal a long, graceful neck. She also had a wide but delicately angled jaw, an expressive mouth, a short, stubborn nose dusted with a handful of freckles and the prettiest slanted golden brown eyes Kit had ever seen. She reminded him of a kitten. A sleek, elegant, very mischievous and playful kitten.

Of course, he reminded himself briskly, she wasn't his type at all.

Plus, he was only going to be here for another hour or so.

Besides, he was allergic to cats.

The woman caught his eye and shrugged helplessly. Kit gave her a don't-worry wave. "Yes, Maisie, I know you're anxious," she said soothingly into the phone, "but I think you'll find it will all work wonderfully. I know what. Come by the shop this afternoon and we'll go over it again. We can review anything you're really in doubt about. Good. Three, then? Great. Bye." Putting down both phone and silver teapot, she stood up.

"Thanks so much for waiting. Can I help you?" she asked.

She was taller than he'd thought, about five foot seven, and slender. Her legs were tanned and slim and endless. Her feet were bare. She had on a short loose dress with a high gathered waist and big yellow buttons up the front. It made him wonder whether the buttons really came undone and what, if anything, was underneath them.

"Yes. I'm looking for Jillian Sanderson," Kit said.

"That's me," the woman said. "But just plain Jilly will do."

Kit frowned. "No. I need Jillian *Mabel* Sanderson," he clarified.

"That's still me. Sorry," she said, confused by his resistance. Suddenly her face cleared. "Oh, my God. Are you from the IRS?"

"Don't be ridiculous," Kit snapped, insulted. "Do I *look* like I'm from the IRS?"

"There's no need to get huffy. I figure only someone from the government would wear a suit and know my name was Mabel. And for the record, I have no idea what IRS men look like."

"They wear wing-tip shoes and polyester shirts. They wear suits," Kit retorted, gesturing at himself, "that do *not* look like this."

God, Jilly thought, marveling, *what a colossal jerk.*

Absolutely drop-dead, to-die-for, star-material gorgeous, but still a jerk.

"Thank you, Beau Brummell," she said aloud. "Now that we have established that you are not the stuffy bureaucrat I still think you dress like, could we get back to business? To repeat: how can I help you?"

Kit closed his eyes in fury. Gathering his wits, he realized that he was not ready to explain Lavinia's bequest to this snotty little hellcat. He needed a minute to regroup. "I'm looking for a gift," he improvised, more boldly than he felt.

"For a woman?" At Kit's nod, Jilly probed further, bracing herself. "A relative? No? Perhaps a...significant other?" *Of course,* she thought, quelling an irrational stab of disappointment. *Well, I hope she appreciates his suit.*

"Uh...yes," Kit said. He'd had plenty of women, but significant was certainly not the word he would have chosen for them. There wasn't even anyone insignificant at the moment. He was sorry he'd ever started this, but there was no backing out now. Doggedly he continued. "That's right. A significant other."

"What is she like?" Jilly asked.

"Like? I don't know," Kit said, caught off guard.

"You want to buy your lady a gift, but you don't know what she's like?" Jilly stared at him. *On second thought,* she decided, *jerk is far too kind. Double jerk? Jerk squared?*

"Yes. No. No, of course I know what she's like. She likes—let's see. Art—and travel—and, that's right, flowers. Loves flowers. She's...beautiful. Proud. Vulnerable," Kit said wildly, cursing himself.

Jeez, Malone. What the hell has gotten into you? he thought. *Five minutes in this shop and you sound like a second-rate soap opera.*

Just wait till she finds out she's inherited you as a business partner. She's going to love it.

Good going, cowboy. Sure glad you're holding the reins.

Jilly turned away from him, rolling her eyes and silently praying for patience. "Okay. Well, that's something," she said with false cheer. Maybe there was some chance of making a sale before one or both of them were carted off to an asylum. The combined impression of this man's devastating looks and lunatic personality made her feel almost dizzy.

"As you can see," she continued, gesturing around the shop, "we have lots of gift ideas. Since she likes flowers, you might consider one of the Victorian needlepoint pillows or a floral watercolor. Perhaps a gift basket of these English bath salts. Or if you want to be a bit more extravagant, this antique writing case is beautiful. Elegant women used to use them for correspondence," Jilly said, opening a glossy wooden box to reveal a nest of inkwells, nib pens and stationery racks. "I love this piece, myself, and the flower painted on the lid is appropriate to your friend's interests. It would be a very special and romantic gift."

Much as it pained him to admit it, Kit thought, Jillian—Jilly—Sanderson was very good at her job. She was tactful about providing options at every price, just the thing to help the typical befuddled male shopper. Hell, she'd convinced him, and he didn't even have the girlfriend he was supposed to be shopping for.

She was, in fact, coming out of this encounter far more successfully than he was. It really annoyed him.

"The writing case," he said. "That looks good to me. How much does it cost?"

"Two hundred and thirty dollars," she said.

"Two *hundred* and thirty dollars," Kit repeated slowly, deliberately condescending. *So there, hellcat,* he thought. "For a couple of old pens in a box? Isn't that a bit high?"

"No. It's a bargain. Sorry," Jilly said, lying. She wasn't sorry, at all. She gritted her teeth. *Quadruple jerk,* she thought. *Jerk supreme.* "It's a unique piece. It's in perfect condition. It has historical as well as artistic value."

How dare this overdressed idiot insult my antiques? she fumed. More to the point, how dare he quibble with her prices? Jilly's temper flared. She threw tact to the winds. "I assumed you were looking for something nice, given that flashy suit you're so anxious to get credit for. But I'm happy to show you something more modest. A single place mat? A handkerchief? A matched pair of beeswax candles? Or perhaps your lady would like this lovely bar of floral soap? Four dollars before tax, and I'll throw in the gift wrap for free."

"On second thought, the writing case will be fine. After all, she's a very special woman," Kit said coolly. It was worth two hundred lousy bucks just to put this babe in her place. "Elegant. Sophisticated. Beautifully turned out. At her best in all situations, of course. Never at a loss."

"Of course. I'm so glad your memory is returning," Jilly cooed.

"Yup. Too bad your manners couldn't make the trip with it," Kit said.

"There's nothing wrong with my manners that your departure won't cure," Jilly snapped. It was heartbreaking, selling a great antique to this loser. "How would you like to pay for this? Check? Credit card? Animal pelts?"

Kit pulled out his wallet and handed her his credit card. "This will do."

Jilly shoved her half-polished silver aside, ran the card through the authorization phone and pulled a receipt from her desk. "Fine. Date, August 16. Item, one antique writing case. Payment, VISA. Gold, of course. Nothing but the best." *Customer, Satan.* "Customer, Christopher Malone." Jilly stared at the imprint on the card. She closed her eyes and tried to count to ten. She made it to four. "Christopher Malone?" she asked.

"That's me," Kit said.

"Christopher 'Kit' Malone? Lavinia Malone's grandson?"

"That's still me. Sorry," Kit said. "Actually, I was going to introduce myself earlier. I didn't really come to buy a gift. We have some more substantial business to discuss."

"I should have known," Jilly said, putting her head in her hands.

Next time you want your life transformed by the unexpected, kiddo, she thought, *just get run over by a truck. It won't be less painful, but it'll be quicker.*

Thanks, Margaret. Thanks, Pankhurst.

Remind me to ruin your lives sometime.

"What should you have known? How? Who told you?" Kit asked aggressively.

"No one. I don't know anything. Never mind," Jilly sighed, resignedly motioning him to a chair. One thing was for sure. Christopher Malone would never understand about her asking favors from a cat.

"I don't believe you," Kit Malone said.

"Of course not," Jilly answered. "You being so up front and all, you should know."

"Very funny. Let's get down to business," Kit said.

"Oh, goody. Let's," Jilly said.

2

JILLY STILL COULDN'T believe it. This man was really Lavinia Malone's grandson? Though, now that she looked more closely, she could see the resemblance in the long bones, the strong jaw, and above all the eyes, widely set and of a gray as clear as a Norwegian fjord.

But Lavinia's features had glowed with wisdom and serenity. Kit Malone's sharp black eyebrows and jutting cheekbones were not serene. His mouth was cutting and his eyes looked cold. You could imagine this man exuberant or angry, but never peaceful. He was arrogant, aggressive and completely self-absorbed. Jilly could well believe that he was as successful as Lavinia had told her. But responsible? Kind? Sensitive, as Lavinia had also claimed? *Puhleeze*, she thought. Ordinarily Lavinia had been a shrewd judge of character, but in Kit's case the golden glow of age or the bliss of shared bloodlines had clearly steered her wrong.

"Okay. First things first," Jilly said. "Do I get to take the writing case back?"

"No," Kit said. "I bought it, and I'm keeping it."

"You don't deserve it."

"Too bad. Brandy does."

"Brandy? Your paragon of female elegance is named Brandy? How old is this person? Eight?"

"Twenty-three," Kit said, shocking himself, "with a great set of you-know-whats." He watched the tip of Jilly

Sanderson's pretty little nose turn pink. Admittedly it was an unnecessarily vulgar remark. But now that he was in control of things again, he was kind of enjoying this. She was pretty cute, as long as a guy held on to the upper hand.

"That's disgusting," Jilly said.

"Right." Kit reached into his jacket pocket for Lavinia's will. "Read this. I think you'll take it better from a piece of paper."

Jilly read. Kit watched her pretty nose get pinker.

When she looked up, she had tears in her big brown eyes.

"I can't believe Lavinia was this generous. It's like we were family," she said. "And I can't believe you're taking it out on me in such a mean, lousy, childish fashion."

"For God's sake. Don't cry," Kit said, shocked. So much for the upper hand. "Have a tissue." He handed her one from the box he sighted on the desk, then sneezed himself.

"Thanks. Gesundheit. Have a tissue," she sniffled.

"Thanks," he said. "What are you talking about? What am I taking out on you?"

"The fact that Lavinia gave me some of your stupid inheritance," she said. "The fact that because of me you're a poorer man. Why else would you be so obnoxious?"

Kit looked at her, befuddled. Just when he thought he'd established some kind of rhythm with her, she'd managed to completely unnerve him again. Suddenly all the hellcat fire was gone. She looked like a drowned kitten. She thought it was his fault. She was completely wrong, so why were her idiotic tears enough to break his heart? "Jillian. Ahem. Jilly," he said in the most tender, comforting tone he could muster with so little practice.

Jilly went on as if he hadn't spoken. "Well, it isn't my fault. I didn't ask for it and I don't want it."

"Jilly," Kit began again, and sneezed.

"No. Don't Jilly me. I'm going to the lawyers tomorrow and giving it back. Stop sneezing," Jilly said tearfully.

"I'm not sneezing for fun," Kit said indignantly, forgetting to be comforting. He sneezed again, loudly.

"My grandmother wanted you to own half of the inn," he continued, "and you're damned well going to own half of it. Even if I have to stand over you with a whip."

"Don't tell me what to do, and don't threaten me, you big bully." Jilly wiped her cheeks, feeling entirely out of control. "Your grandmother liked me. She must have intended to help me. It's not her fault you duped her. She certainly didn't leave me a legacy just so that she could saddle me for life with a controlling, chauvinistic, underevolved cretin."

Kit sneezed.

"Grow up, dimwit," he said. Obviously, his attempts at comfort weren't working. Shock tactics were needed here. "I was not nasty to you because you're taking away my money. I have money to spare, which you would know if you knew anything about me, or Lavinia, or the stock market, or men's clothes, which—based on your crack about the IRS—you obviously don't."

Satisfied, he watched her tragic expression return to the mulish fury he'd grown accustomed to. Good. Now if only he could stop sneezing.

"I was nasty to you," he continued, sniffing and sneezing again, "because you're an uppity know-it-all broad who insulted my tailor."

"Well, that's certainly clear," Jilly said, handing him another tissue. She dabbed at her own damp eyes. "Let me be equally clear, and say that your sneezing is really making me very nervous."

"It would help if you'd stop making comments about it.

Didn't your mother ever teach you not to be personal?" Suddenly Kit was suspicious. "You don't have a cat in this place somewhere, do you?"

Kit Malone's once beautiful gray eyes were almost as red as hers were, Jilly noticed. His bold, disgustingly perfect nose was red, too. The observation made her feel much better. Suppressing a shaky smile, she gestured toward the slipper chair Kit had perched his oversize frame on.

"Yes, I do. Every shop needs a cat. In fact, you're sitting on her, more or less." Jilly bent down and snaked an arm underneath the chair's skirting, fishing out what looked like a huge brown mop.

"My God," Kit said in disbelief, sneezing again. "That's the hairiest thing I've ever seen in my life."

"Pankhurst is a Maine coon," Jilly said sweetly, giving the creature a kiss on what Kit presumed was its head. Even in the depths of his misery he noticed that Jilly's hair and the cat's fur were almost the same color, both composed of what seemed like a thousand different shades of warm, tawny, tortoiseshell brown. "Maine coons are noted for the length and fullness of their fur," she continued perversely, holding up a feathery paw in demonstration. She was beginning to enjoy this. Kit Malone was really quite attractive, as long as a girl held on to the upper hand.

"I don't care if the bloody thing's a rare Siberian ice leopard," Kit said, sniffing. "If you really want me to stop sneezing, could you please get its tufts out of my face?"

"If you wish." Majestically Jilly carried Pankhurst to the lace-curtained French doors at the rear of the shop and dropped the cat into the tiny garden outside. "I'm surprised you have this prissy little allergy, a big macho guy like you," she said as she returned. The hem of her dress brushed his knees as she moved past him. She sat down,

pulling her loosely gathered skirt down toward her knees.
Suddenly she was irrationally aware that however unre-
vealing her clothing was, it still consisted of exactly one
thin cotton dress and one pair of cotton bikini panties.

Stop it, Sanderson, she thought. *You are decently, even re-
spectably clothed. The fact that you're not wearing a bra is irrel-
evant. He can't see that. Even if he could, he wouldn't care. You
are not half-naked.*

Right, she thought. *You just* feel *half-naked.*

Crossing her legs, she tugged at her skirt again. For
good measure, she crossed her arms in front of her chest.

I wish she wouldn't do that, Kit thought. *She's definitely not
wearing a bra. Maybe she's not wearing underpants, either—
maybe that's why she keeps tugging at her skirt. Stop it, Malone.
You are being totally juvenile. You cannot possibly care whether
this woman is wearing underwear.*

Right, he thought. *You just* feel *like you care.*

"Aside from cats, I'm not allergic to anything but gun-
fire. That masculine enough for you? And what kind of
dumb name is Pankhurst, anyway?" Kit said.

"The Pankhursts were a family of Victorian suffragettes.
They led the fight for votes for women and encouraged female activists to hunger strike when they were jailed. Men
tried to intimidate them, but the Pankhurst women never
gave up."

"Great. It figures." Kit leaned his head on the back of the
slipper chair, defeated. Suffragette. Sure. She was a complete and utter nut. And she probably didn't wear underwear, either. Trying to keep the upper hand with Jillian
Mabel Sanderson was like nailing water to a wall. Despite
himself, he could feel a corner of his mouth twitching.

Jilly looked at his slumped form. Fine. So it was a weird
thing to name a cat. Okay, a ridiculous thing to name a cat.
She'd been going through a difficult time when she chose

it. That was nothing, of course, compared to the difficult time she was going through now. She stifled a giggle and tried not to catch his eye.

She caught his eye.

They both burst out laughing.

"I'm going to make some tea," Jilly said when the hilarity had subsided. "My stomach hurts, and I'm exhausted."

"I'll help."

"Absolutely not," she said in alarm. "You'll pick on the way I boil the water or something, and we'll remember that we can't stand each other. We've managed to achieve three whole minutes of truce. Let's go wild and shoot for four."

"OKAY, SANDERSON," KIT said, returning his empty teacup to its saucer. "End of truce. Let's do this."

"Fine," Jilly said. "The peace was too good to last, anyway. What precisely is it that I'm supposed to do?"

"You," Kit said, "are supposed to redecorate Truelove House. I am supposed to watch the money."

"That's not exactly what the will said," Jilly objected. "It said we were supposed to redecorate the place together."

"Don't get picky. Savor your freedom." Kit gave her a forbidding look. "After the renovation, we're just supposed to be joint owners. The fifty-fifty split complicates things a bit, but I'm sure something convenient can be worked out. We can fax each other about any management decisions that arise."

"That would be especially convenient if I had a fax."

"Lavinia's estate will buy you one," Kit said.

What if I don't want one? Jilly thought, but she stayed silent. There would be bigger issues to argue about. She gathered her scattered thoughts. "Luckily the inn itself is in good shape," she said. "I remember a lot of repairs being done last year, and Margaret told me they'd taken care of the major problems. Even so, November 12 gives us only, let's see, over a dozen weeks. We'll need to set up a schedule to hash out the style and colors immediately."

"That won't be necessary," Kit said. "I can give you my input right now. My suggestion is that the new decoration be appropriate."

"Appropriate?"

"Yup. Appropriate." Kit sat back.

"Definitely too good to last. What are you telling me? I'm supposed to redecorate a—what?—thirteen room hotel of which I am, I might remind you, only a 50 percent owner? In a couple of months? And the only insight you're willing to provide is the fact that it should be appropriate? Appropriate to what? Your basic Motel Six? The Ritz-Carlton? A country cottage? A Newport estate? What?"

"Whatever," Kit said.

Jilly just looked at him. So beautiful. So obstinate. It was a shame. She hadn't had to call him a jerk in almost ten minutes.

Kit sighed. She wasn't going to like what he was about to do. It was either going to make her sad or angry. Better angry, he decided. He wasn't sure he could survive another bout of sadness.

"You're going to think this is cold, Jilly, and I'm sorry for that," he said. And he was, sorrier than he could have imagined an hour ago. But it couldn't be helped. "I loved my grandmother, much more than you might think. But as she well knew, I have a business to run two hundred miles away from here. Even if I wanted to—and in all honesty, I don't—I simply can't while away my time in Key West drinking iced tea and chatting about—" he waved a dismissive hand at the shop "—cabbage roses."

Furious again, Jilly glared back into his cool clear eyes.

"You're right. I do think it's cold, Malone. Though I'm not sure why that should surprise me. A man who can't be bothered to attend the funeral of his own grandmother certainly can't be expected to worry about the fine points of doing what she asked in her last will and testament. But more importantly, your attitude makes me professionally uncomfortable. You can't afford to be helpful? Fine. But then I'm sure you can understand that I can't afford to spend weeks of my time and thousands of dollars trying to read your mind. What if you hate what I've done with Truelove House?"

Kit looked calmly at her. "I won't care enough to hate it. The difference between pink walls and blue ones simply isn't going to shake up my universe, hard as that may be for a decorator to believe. I presume Lavinia chose you for a reason. That's enough for me."

"What if I run way over budget or rip you off?"

"You won't," Kit said, amused.

"How can you be so sure?"

His voice was patient. "I know you won't rip me off because my grandmother knew it," he said. "She was a very shrewd lady. Second, I know it because I've checked you out. This morning I talked to three of the other antique dealers in town, who tell me you're honest, and also to two of your clients, who positively gush. And third, I know it because I'm going to be watching you. I said I didn't want to sit around Key West picking wallpaper patterns, not that I didn't want to keep an eye on the business side of things. You're going to make up a proposal. You're going to provide copies of itemized bills. You can rest assured that if I so much as suspect any of your actions to be—shall we say inappropriate?—I'll not only be down here in an instant but if necessary I'll use all the resources at my disposal, and I can assure you they're considerable, to sue the bejesus out of you. Now. Have I covered everything?"

"Splendidly." Jilly stood up, her movements tense and jerky. She felt angry, tired, tense with disappointment. For a few minutes there, while they were sipping their tea, she'd actually thought it would be fun to work with him, despite his high-handed manners and fancy city ways. What was wrong with her? Why didn't she ever learn?

"Don't let me keep you from your appointment with the fast track," she said, reaching under the sales desk for a striped shopping bag. "And here. Be sure to take darling Brandy's gift with you."

"Thank you, Sanderson," Kit said evenly.

"You're welcome, Malone. Good luck on the trip home. You'll need it."

Kit glanced at her, curious. "Luck?" he asked.

"Luck," Jilly answered. She strode to the shop door and held it open. What had been a quiet sun-filled street an hour before was now a river. Rain poured in sheets from Jilly's neat striped awning.

Kit groaned.

"Yes," Jilly said with icy cheerfulness. "If you want to get back to Miami anytime soon, a bit of luck might be in order. Unless, of course, you *like* driving hundreds of miles on a two-lane road in a storm. I presume you've got good tires on, what is it, let me guess—your Porsche?"

"Jaguar," Kit corrected automatically.

"Ah, yes, Jaguar. I should have known. Wonderful cars, though not known for their performance in the rain." The street flashed silver with lightning, the sharp glare followed seconds later by a booming clap of thunder. "Make that thunderstorms."

Kit scowled. Dear Lord. It was too much. Two miserable wasted days away from the office. The disapproval of virtually everyone in Key West. Lavinia's eccentric will. The infuriating, and infuriatingly fetching Jilly Sanderson. A cat with enough fur to induce allergy attacks in the entire Marine Corps. And now a bloody monsoon. "I knew it. This place is cursed," Kit mumbled. "I hate Key West."

Jilly gave him a saccharine smile. "The feeling is mutual," she said. "I don't have an umbrella, but could I interest you in a parasol? Or perhaps that would injure your dignity."

"No, thanks, I'll manage," Kit said grimly as he stepped onto the sidewalk. "And I wouldn't be making jokes about dignity if I were you."

"Why not?"

"Why not?" Kit repeated, pivoting to face her. Suddenly he was standing only inches away from Jilly under the dripping shop awning. The rain made a shimmering transparent wall between the two of them and the world. Jilly was close enough to smell Kit's clean soapy scent and see the tiny variations of gray in his mesmerizing eyes, which were looking straight into hers.

For one long moment he was still, and Jilly thought he was going to kiss her. She stared back at him, shocked by how much she suddenly wanted to be in this under-evolved cretin's perfectly developed arms. Instead, infuriatingly, he simply took one strong finger and drew it over her cheek.

"I wouldn't joke about dignity, Sanderson," he said softly, still staring down at her, "because the entire time I've known you, you've had silver polish all over your pretty, little nose." And turning on his heel, he walked away.

JILLY DROPPED HER TOTE bag on the bedroom rug, kicked off her shoes, flopped on the bed and called her best friend, Belle.

"Hey, kiddo. Can you talk?" she said. "What's happening?"

"Let me just switch phones. Okay. That one had jelly on it. What's happening is the usual. You know," Belle said. "Mess. Disorder. Mayhem. Chaos."

"Known to their friends as Matthew, Nathaniel, Olivia and Katherine."

"The very same," Belle said. Seven years ago, petite, blond, vivacious Belle Lincoln and her handsome husband, Linc, had had boy twins. Four years ago, they had had girl twins. They loved their kids dearly but they were not anxious, Belle vowed, to try again. Belle was Jilly's closest married friend, the confidante who gave her a glimpse of what it was like to be a happy wife and mom. Jilly was Belle's closest unmarried friend, the pal who gave Belle a glimpse, as Belle said, of what it was like to own high heels and sleep through the night.

"Since three o'clock," Belle continued, "I've endured two temper tantrums, three bouts of bickering, one broken Ninja Turtle, one lost Hollywood Barbie, seven I-hate-yous and four you're-not-fairs. I might try exorcism. How are you?"

"I might try exorcism, too."

"Of whom? Maisie DuMaurier? The landlord of the shop?" Belle paused hopefully. "Your dear ex-husband, Claude?"

"Not today," Jilly sighed, twirling the phone's curly cord around her finger pensively. "In her will, Lavinia Malone left me a half share of Truelove House."

"Jilly!" Belle whistled. "That's fabulous. You love that place, and you loved Lavinia."

"Yeah. It's wonderful. It was so generous of her, I can't

quite take it in. Unfortunately Lavinia also seems to have left me a share in her grandson. He owns the other half of the inn."

"The clown who didn't make it to Lavinia's funeral?"

"The very same. You'll notice that he managed to get here for the reading of her will. Charming set of priorities."

"What's he like?"

"Very...male."

"Meaning what? Snores? Likes gadgets? Doesn't want to talk about relationships? What?"

"Meaning overbearing, impatient, judgmental and utterly condescending." *Meaning sexy.*

No. Cut it out. Forget sexy.

"Jilly, hold on. Nathaniel, darn it, cut that out. You are not Paul Bunyan and Olivia is not a tree," Belle said. "Okay, I'm back. Am I detecting true personal antipathy or just your current free-floating dislike of men in general?" she continued.

"Both. Kit Malone is a conceited jerk who makes Donald Trump look like Gandhi, and men in general are not my favorite flavor at the moment."

"They're not so bad, and you know it."

"Stalin was a man. Nero was a man. Caligula. Bluebeard. Ted Bundy. J. Edgar Hoover. The Marquis de Sade." Jilly looked idly around her pretty white bedroom, envisioning J. Edgar Hoover amid its old lace and antique quilts. He wasn't a good fit, true, but he wasn't all that much more unlikely than her ex-husband, F. Claude Henderson, Jr. Now, when it came to Kit Malone.... *No*, she thought hastily, pushing aside the thought of Kit's long, lean body stretched out in her big, soft bed. *He wouldn't fit in, either.*

Hey, what the hell. I'll redecorate.

Stop it, Jilly, she told herself. *Now.*

"Jilly? You there? What about Medea? Lizzie Borden? Leona Helmsley?" Belle countered.

"They had bad fathers. Don't snort," Jilly said. "I mean, men grow hair on their backs. Doesn't that say it all?"

"No. And not all men have hair on their backs," Belle objected. "Linc, for example, is completely smooth."

"Oh, all right." Jilly admitted. "For that matter, Claude, the arch male, didn't have hair on his back."

"He barely had hair on his head."

Jilly giggled. "Belle, that's unkind."

"So was Claude."

"True," Jilly said. "But why does this conversation keep circling back to him? Enough already."

"Pre-cise-ly. Enough already. Our talk circles back to Claude because Claude—or at least his criticisms of you— are still so much on your mind. If you could just get to the point where you could learn to distrust just Claude rather than guys in general, we'd have it made."

"Thank you for sharing," Jilly said. "And here I thought I was going to have to invest in a toll call to Dr. Ruth."

"You can laugh all you want, but I'm right. It's not normal."

"It's not normal to bitch about men?"

"It's not normal for someone as smart and beautiful as you not to at least want to meet someone nice."

Jilly sighed. "I do, too, want to meet someone nice. Just not yet. Let's change the subject."

"So, seriously. What about this Malone? Oops, wait a minute." Jilly could hear Belle talking to the kids. "Sorry. Is he young? Cute? Rich?"

Jilly considered her answer. "I'm not sure that's a change of subject. But his name is Christopher, he's young-ish, and he's definitely rich. As for cute, well, you would

probably say so. But cute is not the word I would personally use about Kit Malone." *Try gorgeous. Hot. Generally
devastating.*

Try domineering. Materialistic. Self-absorbed. Taken.

"I have to see him for dinner tonight, to go over the
plans for the inn," Jilly finished.

"Ah. How...interesting."

"Like surgery without anesthesia."

"Well," Belle said practically, "if it's going to be so miserable, why did you agree to go?"

"You know, Belle," Jilly confessed, "I have no idea. I
met him this morning and we hated each other on sight. I
was so surprised when he called about dinner that I said
yes before I could stop myself." Kit's call had caught her in
the middle of a restless afternoon. Since he was stuck in
Key West, he had said in his arrogant, unconsciously se-
ductive voice, he would be willing to listen to any propos-
als she had to make about the inn over dinner. If she had
any ideas. If she was still so very anxious to get his input.
And if, of course, she didn't already have plans, he'd
added in a tone which implied that she hadn't had dinner
plans since childhood. She had never been Miss Popularity, but it wasn't the most gracious invitation she'd ever re-
ceived. It wasn't even close. She had opened her mouth to
say no.

And said yes. Sure. Ernest's. At seven.

"Where are you going to take him?" Belle asked.

"Ernest's."

"Ernest's? That's a little...downscale, isn't it? Will he
like it?"

"He'll loathe it," Jilly said happily.

"Great. I can see that this is shaping up to be the kind of
evening memories are made of. What are you going to
wear?" Belle asked.

"I was thinking armor," Jilly answered, and hung up.

KIT DROPPED HIS BRIEFCASE on the floor of the Truelove Inn's only available bedroom, kicked off his shoes, flopped on the bed and called Jilly Sanderson.

He wasn't sure why he wanted to see her again. Even the fact that a thunderstorm raged outside and he was stuck in Key West for another night didn't explain it. In the scant hour they'd been together she'd somehow managed to irritate him, anger him and humiliate him. She'd made him feel like a coldhearted son of a bitch, a lothario and, worse, a fool.

She'd also made him feel...alive. Being with Jilly Sanderson was an energetic experience, kind of like a good game of squash or a profitable session trading penny stocks. You had to pay attention with Jilly. If your mind wandered for even a minute, like to the intriguing buttons on her dress, her mood changed and you were lost. Given that most of the women he dated were about as lively as pet rocks, it was a novelty. *Exactly*, he thought. *A novelty. It'll wear off. It always does.*

You hope.

The plans with Jilly set, Kit called Henry Weinstein, his partner. Henry was exactly Kit's age and exactly six inches shorter. He was skinny and sensible. His voice squeaked. And he tended to get anxious when Kit was away.

"Hank? Kit."

"Jeez, Kit. Finally. It's four-thirty. Where have you been?"

"Taking care of my grandmother's will. You know that. Did Angus MacPherson call? What's happening with the market?"

"Angus MacPherson did not call. Obviously the compelling logic of your sales pitch escaped him. The rumor is he's talking to those finks at Capital Management. And what do you mean, what's happening with the market? Do you mean you don't know?" Henry squeaked.

"No. I don't know. The stock ticker that I had surgically implanted in the left side of my rib cage seems to have malfunctioned. Cut it out."

"Fine. Everything's peachy. The Dow dropped 60 points. NASDAQ, too. And Allied Technologies lost a whopping 12 points. We're getting creamed, Malone."

Kit sat up straighter. "Really? Great."

"Great? Great." Henry's voice rose again.

"Hank," Kit said patiently, "do not yell. It is not actually necessary for everyone in the state of Florida to hear you unassisted. That's the point of a phone."

"I know what the point of a phone is, Malone. I have spent the entire goddamned day with a receiver stuck in my ear, trying to reassure your clients that they're not going to end up in debtors' prison."

"Our clients, Hank, remember? We share them. I make them money, and you schmooze them. So go ahead. Schmooze them. Comfort them. Reassure them."

"I have nothing reassuring to say. You own Allied. I own Allied. The pension fund of United Manufacturing, which happens to be our biggest client, owns Allied." Hank paused. "*Lots* of Allied."

"We're all big boys. We can tolerate a little risk."

"Kit, for God's sake, the lady who takes care of our office plants owns Allied."

"Now that's a problem. Clients come and clients go, but I can't live without my schefflera." Kit pulled his laptop computer out of his briefcase and tinkered for a moment. "Right. Here's what we'll do. You'll tell your personal banker and the people at United and Mattie the plant lady not to worry, and I'll buy us all 10 percent more Allied stock when the market opens tomorrow."

"Kit," Henry said mournfully, "have I reminded you recently how much I dislike it when you do this?"

"Henry," Kit answered, "have I reminded you recently that you have an expensive car, an expensive condo, an expensive boat and an expensive fiancée because I do this?"

"Also an expensive ulcer. I'm saving up for an even more expensive coronary. I figure I can swing it by Christmas. Maybe earlier, if this keeps up. When the *Wall Street Journal* nicknamed you Killer, they had no idea how literally they were speaking."

Kit grinned. When Hank's sense of humor returned, it meant the worst was over. "I'll be back tomorrow by ten."

"Eight-thirty."

"Nine-thirty. That's final. It's a three-hour drive. You can stave off any riots by yourself for a measly half hour, Hank."

"You were supposed to be back this afternoon," Hank said.

"I know. My grandmother's will was a little bit more complicated than I expected."

If you called Jilly Sanderson a complication.

"Nine-thirty. No later. Don't worry, Hank. I have a feeling about this one."

"You've been wrong before."

"I know. That's what makes this fun."

Hank snorted. "Yeah. I haven't had so much fun since the last time I fell out of a tenth-story window. This is not fun, Kit. This is gut-wrenching terror. People's futures are at stake here. Big-time. Including ours."

"Okay, then. Fine. So it's not fun. It's necessary." Kit wandered across his room to the window overlooking the inn's back garden and fiddled with the shutter so that he could see outside. *Needs work,* he diagnosed, looking absently down at the dense rain-lashed beds and paths.

"No," Hank said. "It used to be necessary. When we were just starting out, trying to get ourselves established, it was necessary. We needed a track record. We needed to make a killing on every stock we bought. We needed you to get written up in the *Wall Street Journal.* But now we've built a reputation. We don't need to hit a home run every single time anymore. We could occasionally, just occasionally afford to hit your basic grounder to left field."

Be a great place to make love in, that garden, Kit thought. He had a sudden confused image of a garden bench and a beautiful woman and moonlight, followed by an even more confused image of the yellow buttons on Jilly Sanderson's dress. Exasperated with himself, he pulled his mind back to the present. "Well," he said peevishly, "maybe *you* don't need to hit a home run, and *we* don't need to hit a home run. But *I* need to hit a home run."

"Yeah, but why, is what I'm asking. Because something else is missing, that's why."

Kit closed the shutters and strolled back to the bed, sighing. "Hank, have you seen Brenda lately?"

"My fiancée, Brenda? Yesterday. Why?"

"Because every time you see Brenda you hit me with this something's-missing-from-poor-Kit's-life crap."

"This is not about my relationship with Brenda, kiddo. But at least I *have* a relationship. You've had better relationships with pasta dinners than you've had with women. Okay, my thing with Brenda's not perfect. But there's something there. Something which helps me cope with the fact that I'm almost forty and I'm not gonna win the Nobel Prize for economics and I've got a bald spot the size of a salad plate. Something that saves me from having to take every risk in the book just to prove myself."

"I love it when you get all earnest."

"Go ahead, joke."

"Hank, I know what you're talking about, okay? And part of me accepts what you're saying. But the other part of me hasn't met the right woman yet. And I'm not gonna concoct a so-called relationship with some bimbo just to, quote unquote, have something in my life."

"Nobody's asking you to. But you're not looking in the right places for a relationship. Great sex, yes. Relationships, no."

"You're right. I'm gonna start targeting world-hunger organizations, therapy groups and Mensa meetings the minute I get back. Maybe Mother Teresa is free next Friday night." Kit made a face at the phone receiver. "However, if it makes you happier, I am having a date, more or less, with a very smart and successful woman tonight. Cute, too, in a totally non-bimbo way." *True, she's the most volatile thing this side of Krakatoa and she really hates me. But hey, nobody's perfect.*

"Who is this?"

"The new co-owner of my grandmother's bed-and-breakfast inn. Lavinia left 50 percent of it to me and 50 percent of it to a friend of hers. An antique dealer," Kit explained.

"You're dating a woman with an IQ over sixty? That's good. Straight fifty-fifty split? Co-ownership of an operating business? In an industry with narrow profit margins? That's bad, real bad. Delays. Disagreements. Possible deadlock," Henry said sympathetically. "Problems all around."

"Buddy, you don't know the half of it."

3

JILLY'S FAVORITE MEMBERS of the Conch volleyball team were sitting at the bar in Ernest's arguing, as usual.

"Hey, Jilly!" Larry called.

"Jilly girl," Ned yelled. "Wanna sit over here with us?"

"Look, gang, it's Jilly 'Big Serve' Sanderson," Jeff said. "Whatcha doing here, Jilly? You're not usually a Tuesday night bar bird."

Jilly regarded her three big, burly pals with affection. The Key West volleyball league not only guaranteed her a healthy weekly bout of killer exercise, it gave her a cheering section. Her fellow Conch Team members were a fan club, a therapy group, a support system.

A substitute family, her own being unfortunately unavailable on account of being pretentious fools.

She liked the guys so much she was even willing to suspend her distrust of men on their behalf.

"Greetings, sports fans," she said. "I'm here because I'm having dinner with a suit," she said.

"Business or pleasure?" Larry asked.

"Definitely business," Jilly answered. "The suit in question is navy blue and goes with a maroon-striped silk tie, a gold collar pin and those loafers with the little tassels on them."

"Gucci," Ned said wisely. "Gruesome." Ned, like virtually everyone else in the bar, was wearing clothing the average boat person would have burned on sight.

"City type?" Jeff said.

"Yup," Jilly said. "Miami. Biscayne Bay, to be exact."

"Yuck," the three men said in unison.

"Seriously, guys," Jilly said. "This could get heavy, and I need you to come to my aid. I'd sure appreciate it if you'd drop over once in a while and lighten things up, okay?"

Getting the men's enthusiastic assent—there was nothing the Conch Team liked better than puncturing the self-confidence of a mainlander, unless it was beating the crap out of their arch rivals, the Lobster Team—Jilly strolled to her table, surveying the interior of Ernest's with satisfaction. Ernest's was named for Ernest Hemingway, one of Key West's most famous past residents. The old wooden walls were hung with faded book jackets and posters. Scents of blackened mahimahi and conch fritters wafted enticingly from the kitchen. A smattering of Key West's most eccentric and disreputable residents were hanging out at the bar, talking at the top of their lungs. There were no tourists that Jilly could see. Ernest's was strictly for the locals.

Ernest's was casual, tolerant, unpretentious and bohemian. The perfect place to meet Kit Malone for dinner.

It would drive him nuts.

So, she hoped, would her outfit.

He liked sophistication and polish. He'd probably wear a tie, for God's sake. Jilly, on the other hand, was perfectly dressed for an evening in Key West. Her snug jeans were worn to velvet softness and boasted a huge hole in one knee. Her beloved hot pink Conch Team volleyball shirt was equally tattered and about four sizes too big, allowing it to slip provocatively off one shoulder. Her only concessions to feminine artifice were a pair of gold hoop earrings, a quick coat of lip gloss and a hearty spray of White Linen.

Jilly leaned back in her rattan armchair with satisfaction. In Key West, this was as close to armor as you could get.

At least she didn't have silver polish on her nose. And tonight she would have time to prepare herself, she thought as she ordered a diet soda. She was ten whole minutes early. He wouldn't be able to drop in on her unawares.

"Hello, Jilly," that deep voice said from a foot away.

"Hi, Kit," she answered weakly.

Damn. Once again his presence surprised her. So did his appearance. Somewhere he'd scrounged up a black long-sleeved polo shirt, the kind with a little row of buttons descending temptingly from the neck, and a pair of black jeans almost as worn as her own. The jeans weren't unduly tight, but they managed to prove definitively that he had impossibly narrow hips and utterly beautiful thighs. The shirt wasn't tight, either, but it was perfectly draped over his broad shoulders, tucked casually into his jeans and rolled up at the elbows to reveal elegant, muscular forearms.

Far from looking out of place in Ernest's, Kit Malone looked right at home. He looked lazy and confident and careless and dangerous. In fact, he was the incarnation of everything that was swashbuckling and piratical about Key West.

Not to mention being the most breathtakingly sexy man Jilly had ever seen.

You probably have hair on your back, Malone, she thought. *And boy, would I like to find out.*

Visit Miami, Jilly, she told herself. *You can ask Brandy.*

"Lovely weather we're having," Kit said.

In the few hours since he'd seen her she'd been constantly on his mind, yet he'd still managed to underestimate the supple beauty of her body and the impish delicacy of her features. Her defiantly unladylike clothes just emphasized her femininity. She made him feel almost predatory, but also—more surprisingly for him—protective. First, he fantasized, he'd like to beat all the ogling guys in the bar senseless. Then, he'd like to do the exact same things they probably wanted to do. Kiss her beautifully shaped mouth until her lips got hot and swollen. Slide his fingers underneath the tattered hole in her jeans and stroke her silky thigh. Slip that ridiculously oversize shirt off her beautiful tan shoulder and taste the warm skin beneath.

Terrific, Malone, he thought. *Two minutes, and you're already licking her breasts. The only way you're ever going to get the upper hand with this woman is to put her in a nun's habit.*

Then again, Jilly Sanderson in a nun's habit...

"You look gorgeous, Jilly," he said, sitting down.

Jilly felt her cheeks flush. "That's not funny. Don't jeer at me."

"Jeer?" Kit was dumbfounded. "Why would you think I'm jeering at you?"

Jilly gestured at herself. "Obviously you're used to something a little more...polished." *Remember Brandy, bozo?* "This isn't exactly haute couture."

"Pastrami isn't porterhouse steak, but that doesn't mean it doesn't taste good."

"Gee, thanks, I think. I've never been compared to a cut of meat before."

Kit's reply was interrupted by the arrival of Ned, beaming. At her—and at Kit Malone, who obviously met with his full approval.

"Hey, Jilly," he said. "The suit cancel?"

"Yes," Jilly said weakly. This was really not going as she'd planned. "Last minute change of schedule. Ned Winston, meet Kit Malone."

"Great to meet you," Ned said. "Play volleyball, by any chance?"

"Not recently," Kit said. "I had a decent spike in college."

"Kit's only here for the evening, Ned," Jilly said quickly. This dinner was going to be hard enough without guy talk. "I think Larry needs you. Yup, he's gesturing... In fact, he looks frantic."

"Oh. Really? Okay. Nice to meet you, Kit. Bye, babe," Ned said, ambling away.

"You had plans with someone else for tonight?"

"Yes. He had to cancel. It was too bad," Jilly said. "You would have loved him."

Kit sighed. "Well. Not to return to a sore subject, but I'm sorry if I wasn't clear about my...admiration before. The crack about steak wasn't the most elegant of analogies, but you know what I mean. You're a very beautiful woman, Jilly. I can't imagine that you don't know it."

Sure. My husband thought I was gorgeous—that's why he never let an hour go by without telling me what I needed to fix. And I bet good old Brandy looks just like me. Their cocktails arrived, and Jilly took a grateful gulp of her gin and tonic. "Kit, let's not argue about it. Let's pretend to be normal people and make ordinary uninteresting conversation. Tell me about Miami. I visit the city on buying trips, but I don't know much about it."

"Not much to tell," Kit said smoothly. His gray eyes glinted, but to Jilly's relief he seemed willing to follow her lead into more neutral conversational territory. "It's fast paced and full of contradictions. It's a Southern city with the edge and drive of New York. Very exciting, and sometimes very frustrating."

"Where did you grow up?"

"My father—Charlie, Lavinia's son—grew up in Key

West, but I spent my childhood moving around the East Coast. I went to college at Yale, spent a year or so in Laguna Beach and finally moved to Miami."

"So where do you live now? Right in Miami?" Jilly asked. *So far, so good,* she thought. If they could just manage to talk about geography for two solid hours, everything would be fine.

"I have an apartment not far from my office. It has a great view, and it's all very stark and modern." He raised his drink to her and gave her a lazy grin. "You'd hate it."

"Probably," Jilly admitted. "I'm not the stark-and-modern type. Nor the city type, for that matter."

"Have you ever tried it?"

"I spent most of my life in Atlanta. I only moved to Key West four years ago." Exactly a week after her excruciating divorce from Claude Henderson was final, but she wasn't going to tell Kit Malone that.

Luckily at that moment Jeff strolled up.

"Hey, Jilly," he said brightly, "great to see you."

"Yeah," Jilly said without enthusiasm. "Great. Jeff Davison, meet Kit Malone."

"Hi, Jeff," Kit said. He made an educated guess. "I had a decent spike in college. You do play volleyball, right?"

"Yeah," Jeff said. "With Sanderson, in fact. Sanderson here has the best serve in the league. She really keeps 'em scrambling."

"Oh, I'll just bet she does," Kit said, grinning.

"Well, just stopped by to say hi, but you seem to being doin' fine. See you later, kids."

"Just for the record, how many more of these extraordinarily huge guys are gonna just happen to stop by to check me out?" Kit asked when he was gone.

"Just one. I hope. They're kind of protective. Sorry. I

could always go over to the bar and head Stooge Number Three off at the pass."

"Hell, no," Kit said. "I'm getting a kick out of them."

"Why?"

Because they're making you so rattled. "Because I like them. They like you. They're nice guys."

"Larry is a mailman. Jeff is a fisherman. Ned does things with valves and pipes. They make less money combined than you spent on that famous suit of yours, and they share none of your values."

"I didn't say I would hire them. I didn't say I would marry them. I said I liked them." Kit grinned affectionately at Jilly, who was rubbing her forehead as though she had a headache. She had so many emotions, which kept breaking through her attempts at reserve like sun through cloud. She was so cute. She deserved a break, he thought kindly. "So. Why did you come to Key West?" he asked when their order had been placed.

"Chance, really." Jilly gathered her wits. "I started a decorating business in Atlanta and one of my clients asked me to do his vacation home here. It was love at first sight." Insecure and exhausted from the relentless criticism of Claude, her parents and all of their so-called friends, she'd responded instantly to the relaxed, unjudgmental life-style of the islands. But she wasn't going to tell Kit Malone that, either.

The things she wasn't about to tell Kit Malone could fill an entire conversation. A much more interesting conversation than the one they were having, actually.

"I needed...a change," she said. Kit sensed the hurt behind her words. It pained him just to glimpse it, but after this morning's fireworks it definitely wasn't time to probe.

"Key West is a good place for my business," she continued. "There's enough tourism to keep the shop alive and enough wealthy winter residents to keep me in decorating clients. And I became fascinated with the place, with its wildlife and history. But you've been here often, visiting Lavinia. So you know all about that."

Kit matched honesty for honesty. "Not really, I have to admit. I've visited a lot, sure, but I always tended to stay for a night or two and then go straight back to Miami. Places like the Keys aren't really my thing. They're too loose, too relaxed. Tough for someone of my...compelling personality to handle."

"The island's lazy appearance is a little misleading," Jilly said. She wasn't going to touch the subject of Kit Malone's compelling personality with the proverbial ten-foot pole. "Ever since the seventeenth century, it's been a haven for pirates and Spanish adventurers and wreckers...for scoundrels and treasure seekers of all kinds, really."

"Aha. My disgustingly capitalistic interest suddenly awakens."

"Mmm. For a while the salvage business was so profitable that Key West had the most wealth per capita in America. Not to mention all the illegal profits. Kit Malone, pirate of the stock market, should feel right at home here," Jilly teased. They'd gotten through most of dinner without actually screaming at each other, she thought. Hopefully she could risk a little joke.

"Right. Electronic plunder and corporate plank walking our specialties," Kit joked comfortably back. "Meanwhile, what about coffee or some dessert? I wouldn't mind something soothing and cold."

"Me, too. And tea would be good."

Jilly paused, unsure of what to say. She hated to ruin the pleasant, undemanding mood they'd finally established, and a discussion of their hotly disputed business would probably destroy it in three minutes flat. At the same time, things were getting a little too friendly. It wasn't any wiser to let things go farther with Kit Malone, the dangerous man, than it was with Kit Malone, the evil business partner.

Ruin your evening or ruin your life, Sanderson, she thought. *Your choice.*

Reluctantly she got ready to bring up Truelove House.

"Oops. Moe's on the way—or is it Curly?" Kit said before she could open her mouth.

"Hey, Jilly," Larry said, beaming at her. "Long time no see."

"Larry DellaGuardia, Kit Malone." Jilly gave up. It was hopeless. "Kit had a decent spike in college."

"Really?" Larry said happily. "Do you play now? We could use somebody really tall."

"I'm a touch rusty, but nothing a little practice wouldn't fix. I wouldn't mind trying. Maybe I'll give you a call when I come back to Key West," Kit said.

"Great. I'll look forward to it. See you at the game, Sanderson." Larry pivoted toward the bar. Behind Kit's back, he gave Jilly a thumbs-up signal.

Over Kit's head, Jilly gave him a cold look.

"Wow," Kit said. "That look could freeze lava."

"He seemed to like you. I don't want him to start liking you. I don't want him to get hurt. When are you ever going to be back in Key West, much less playing volleyball?"

"You never know. I'm having fun here. Aren't you?"

"No," Jilly said.

"No? Why not?"

Because you're totally at home here, and you're not supposed to be. Because you're acting nice, and you're not supposed to be nice, either. Because it makes it too hard to hate you, but I do.

I hate you so much I want you to kiss me. Hard.

And because that's never going to happen.

"I'm not having fun," Jilly said desperately, "because I didn't come here to have fun. I came here to talk about the inn."

"Inn, inn, inn," Kit said, "that's all you think about. Smell the flowers, Jilly."

"Cut the crap, Kit. Five hours ago you were so anxious to finish our business and get out of here, you practically left tread marks on my face."

"Things change," Kit said, looking at her.

"The fact that you annoy me is a thing that will endure forever," Jilly snapped.

Kit put down his coffee cup and held up his hands. "Okay. Okay. Don't shoot. I surrender. We'll talk about the inn. What do you want to do? Shaker with a faint hint of English country house? Deco with a French provincial twist?"

Jilly looked at him for a long moment. She lined up her knife and fork, folded her napkin and rearranged her water glass. When she spoke, her voice was grave. "Time out, Kit. One of the reasons I am not having fun with you is that every single time the subject of my career comes up you make some totally dismissive demeaning remark."

Kit frowned. "No. Really? That can't be true. Actually I'm very impressed with how you handle your business."

"When exactly did you share that admiration? Was it before the crack about the writing case, which implied that my merchandise is overpriced? Or after the crack about the cabbage roses, which implied that my entire profession is useless feminine time filler, unworthy of your respect or even your tolerance?"

Kit looked at her serious face. No woman had ever spoken to him in quite that way. She was clearly angry, but she wasn't being mean. She was hurt, but she wasn't trying to wring his pity. She wasn't irrational or catty or weak. She was just...right.

"I'm sorry, Jilly." He reached over and touched her arm, the most fleeting of touches. "I tend to let my smart mouth run away with me. This decorating thing, I was just...I don't know. Stupid. Macho. It was a way of cutting you down to manageable size, I guess. Of keeping the upper hand."

"Kit," Jilly said, "I understand that you want to have the upper hand. I want to have the upper hand, too. The problem is that Lavinia left us fifty-fifty partners. And in a fifty-fifty partnership, no one really ever has the upper hand, at least not for long. We're both just going to have to learn to live with that."

"Yeah. Okay," Kit said. "It does go against my grain, I have to admit. Maybe that's why Lavinia concocted this scheme, to teach me a lesson. But I'm willing to try, if you are."

"All right, then. The inn." Jilly leaned over to turn Kit's wrist so that she could see his watch. She could feel the pulse beneath his warm skin. "This is very preliminary, and it will only take ten minutes. For ten minutes you have to forget your assumption that interior decoration is some dopey extravagance that has nothing to do with the business of Truelove House. For ten minutes you have to try to understand that interior decoration *is* Truelove House, that it defines the kind of emotional experience guests have there, whether they feel relaxed and at home, whether they have fun. Most of all, whether they tip well and come back and send their friends. It has everything to do with all the stuff you love, the profit and the loss. Right?"

"Right," Kit said. What she said made sense. She understood her job, that was for sure. "Go for it."

Jilly finished in nine minutes flat.

Kit leaned back in his seat, searching for words that would convey his reactions to her without his usual flippancy. "Well," he said awkwardly.

He's tongue-tied, Jilly thought, more dismayed than she wanted to admit. *This man is never, ever tongue-tied. He hates it.*

"I love it," Kit said. "That is, I'm very impressed. It all seems clear and realistic to me. Creative, too. It's terrific work, given that you've only had a couple of hours to think about it. But do you really want to do so much of the work yourself? We have enough money for more help."

"No." Jilly shook her head. "There's not enough time to get all of the craftspeople I want, in the time frame Lavinia gave us. Besides, this is more than just a job. This project is special to me, special to Lavinia. I want to be a real part of it, not just a glorified supervisor."

"Fine, then. I'll talk to Ben Knowles, Lavinia's lawyer, about the money."

"Uh, Kit?" Jilly said.

"Yes?"

"I feel…nervous. Like you're humoring me. Are you just saying all this to be nice?"

Kit smiled into her uncertain eyes. "Jilly…remember me? Kit Malone? The—what was it—underevolved cretin? I'm not the guy who tells lies to be polite. I'm the guy who makes mean cracks that hurt people."

"Oh. I remember." Jilly grinned. "Sorry. The speed of your trip from Neanderthal boor to sensitive nineties male got me jetlagged there for a minute."

"Dizzying mood swings do seem to be our specialty," Kit agreed. "Just as well I have to get back to Miami, so we can both get some rest," he added, lying.

Yeah, right, Jilly thought. *I personally am going to sleep like*

*a log tonight. I'm certainly glad you won't be rolling around in
my bed distracting me from the pure pleasure of my insomnia.*

Yeah, right, Kit thought. *Sitting around thinking about licking your breasts is going to be much more relaxing in Miami
than it is here. Sure.*

They walked out of Ernest's in silence.

THE RAIN HAD STOPPED by the time they left the restaurant.
A heavy yellow moon hung over the harbor, and the damp
branches of the mimosa trees scented the cooling air.

"I'll walk you home," Kit said.

"There's no need. I'm just a block or two away, on Car-
oline Street," Jilly answered hastily. As was typical of her
encounters with Kit Malone, this evening had gotten completely out of hand. It was enough excitement for a lifetime. She was scared of the newly likable and sensitive Kit
Malone and terrified of herself. Strolling through one of
the world's most romantic places in moonlit darkness was
not going to help.

"It's no problem. I want to make sure you get home
safely." Kit's voice was curt. With the business of the evening over and the unabashed scrutiny of Jilly's volleyball
pals left behind, there was nothing left to distract him from
her powerfully feminine presence at his side.

Yes, she was irritating and volatile and stubborn as hell.
No, she wasn't his type. But she was something else: his
match, his equal. She was also beautiful, in a way that had
grown on him every hour he watched her. She was such a
mixture of strength and vulnerability. And so innocent of
her own attraction. Innocence wasn't a quality Kit had
ever sought. The women he dated knew their own power,
and they used it. Their imperviousness to real hurt was
part of their appeal for him. But Jilly was different, in a
way he couldn't quite explain.

They walked to Jilly's house in continued silence. Occasionally she felt Kit's warm hand taking her elbow to help her dodge the mirrorlike puddles left by the rain. Jilly paused at the stone gatepost at the front of her small property.

"This is it," she said brightly.

"Oh." Kit glanced at the house. It had a pretty pink front door lit by a small etched glass lamp. The tiny yard brimmed with flowers. "Looks like a nice place."

"It's a shotgun house, one of the homes built by the Conch settlers," Jilly said nervously, hoping Kit wouldn't notice that she wasn't inviting him in. "It's not too convenient, but the neighbors are sweet, and I love it." *God, Jilly, stop talking,* she thought. *You sound like Chatty Cathy.*

"Nice," Kit repeated. *God, Malone, say something else.*

"Well, good night," Jilly said. "We'll be in touch, right? About the inn, I mean. Thanks for a—nice—dinner."

A glint of the old devilish humor sparked in Kit's eyes. To hell with nice. He knew what he was about to do wasn't wise, but this had been way too eventful a day to end with "nice." "Yes, Jilly," he said silkily. "We'll be in touch."

Swiftly, before she could protest, he reached for her, clasping her waist and lifting her in one quick motion until she sat on the top of the waist-high gatepost. Perched there, she was exactly as tall as he was. Hands still possessively claiming her waist, he leaned forward and kissed her, kissing her jaw and cheek and mouth, inhaling her perfume, nuzzling against the softness of her skin. He slid one hand underneath her glossy tumble of hair and cupped her head to pull her near him, wordlessly urging her closer. Teasingly he trailed the fingers of his other hand down her hip toward her thigh, reaching with a sure, dancing touch under the frayed tear in her jeans, stroking her warm and quivering skin. Deliberately he kept the kiss shallow, barely opening his lips against hers, tasting her, teasing her. Trying to let her know how beautiful, how luscious he found her. Trying to beg forgiveness for their fights earlier that day. Giving her time to trust and to respond.

To Jilly, Kit's embrace felt heated, liquid, sensual, overwhelming. She could feel the strength of his shoulders, the pounding of his heart, the muscular solidity of his torso and thighs. Shyly, she opened her mouth against the slightly stubbled skin of his cheek, tasting the clean saltiness of him. The tightness of his clasp made her achingly aware that only two thin layers of fabric separated her breasts from the hard breadth of his chest. Her shirt slipped off her shoulder and she let it fall, wanting him to reach beneath it, wanting him to know that she wore nothing underneath. Instinctively she brought her arms down to clasp the hard curve of his back and curled one leg around his thigh, nestling herself closer to his warmth. His touch was firm, almost rough, and yet it made no demands on her, left her wanting more. In his arms Jilly felt more feminine, more desirable, than she'd ever felt before. More conscious of the masculinity of another body and the softness of her own. More open. More bold, more wanton.

Suddenly more alone.

Reality hit her with the force of a runaway train.

In one fluid motion she pushed him away and for good measure punched him in the stomach.

Kit barely noticed the blow, which glanced off the hard muscles of his abdomen. But the shock of the moment hurt.

"Jesus, Jilly," he gasped. "What was that?"

"Damn you, Kit Malone," she said, yanking her top back up onto her shoulder, her voice shaken. "You walk into my shop without so much as the courtesy of a call.

You ask for my help in buying an expensive present for a girlfriend who—you make sure to let me know—is half my age and twice my bra size. You make a point of telling me how little time you have to spare for me or your grandmother or anything this island stands for. Then you buy me a cheap dinner, turn on the charm and expect me to fall into your arms. Maybe that's how you do things in sophisticated fast-paced Miami. Maybe your women don't care what you do as long as you listen to them talk and toss them a compliment or two. But that's not how it works with me."

"Jilly—" *Damn it*, Kit cursed to himself. In the pleasure of her nearness, he'd forgotten all about this morning's little invention. *Damn* it. "Jilly—"

"No. I don't want to hear it. *No.*" Jilly was adamant. When he had something to gain, Kit Malone had a way with words—she'd certainly found that out. But she'd already heard enough.

"Jilly," Kit ground out, grabbing for her arm in an attempt to keep her still.

Jilly slid off the gatepost and out of his grasp. "Don't you dare paw me," she panted. "I'll do what I promised for the inn. It's what Lavinia wanted, and I'm not letting you stop me from giving it to her. But I don't want to talk to you more than is absolutely necessary. And I don't want to see you." She strode up the walk to her front door, fumbling for the key. "And don't you ever," she called over her shoulder, "*ever* touch me again."

Kit watched helplessly as she slammed the pretty pink door behind her.

THE SUN WAS SHINING the next morning when Jilly awoke. Groggily she levered herself out of her high brass bed and wandered down the hallway stairs. Her head pounded, aching from an unsettled night, echoing with the ugly scene with Kit Malone.

Well, it serves you right, she thought sourly. *You knew exactly what he was, right from the start, and you let yourself ignore it.*

You don't need excitement. You need to have your head examined.

Well, at least she'd sent him away in no uncertain terms. After that scene, he wasn't about to come back. Brandy had probably never looked better to him.

Granted, she felt absolutely wretched, she thought, as a single tear rolled down her cheek. But at least he wasn't here to see her weep. She had cried more since she met Kit Malone than she had in the whole decade before. It was like she was melting or something.

What she needed was to get back into her ordinary routine. That would make her feel better. Another tear rolled down her nose and she ignored it. She needed a hot shower, some good fresh coffee, a just-baked croissant, the *Island Inquirer* crossword and the soothing sunlit warmth of her back garden. Wiping yet another tear off her chin, she opened her front door to pick up her paper.

The newspaper rested neatly on her porch's deep green floor. Next to it sat a familiar gift bag from her shop, its handles still tied with her signature striped ribbon.

Stuffed into the top of the bag were a bunch—a clump— of roses, beautiful tightly furled shell pink blooms still damp from dew and trailing with leaves, broken stems, even a filament or two of root.

Stuck among the flowers was a note, scrawled in a bold slanted hand on Truelove House letterhead.

Dear Jilly,
I'm more sorry than you can imagine for my thought-

lessness yesterday night. I just got carried away. I'm probably just as self-absorbed and heartless as you say. But please believe me when I say that I have no girlfriend. When I found out about Lavinia's will I wanted to see how you do business. I needed an excuse to watch you sell me something and that idiotic Brandy story was the best I could do on the spur of the moment. It was stupid, and it turned out to be cruel, too, but it seemed logical at the time.

Anyway, there was no other woman—in my mind, in my life or anywhere else—when I kissed you last night. That's the simple truth.

Kit

P.S. Please accept the gift. I think it's perfect for you. Throw it or give it away if you must, but remember I paid for it. If you put it back into the shop I'll deck you. And believe me, I *will* find out.

P.P.S. It's 5:00 a.m. and I have to leave for Miami. The florists aren't open, so I picked the flowers from the yard two doors down from yours. Hope your neighbors are really as sweet as you think.

Jilly stood on the stoop and read the note again, shaking her head in disbelief. It was classic Christopher Malone. Confident. No, arrogant. Obnoxious. Funny. Honest—the note perfectly explained his bumbling foolishness in the shop, his awkwardness when he was trying to describe his so-called girlfriend. And with a completely unexpected edge of tenderness, a surprising willingness to admit he was wrong.

Kit Malone was the most devastatingly confusing person Jilly had met in a long time. Maybe ever.

"Bye-bye, Brandy," she said aloud. "I know this is hard

to believe, but I don't know what I'm going to do without you."

She picked up the newspaper, bag and sopping wet roses and went inside.

"As for you, Lavinia," she continued, "I'm trying to trust you. But I hope you know what you're doing."

If she didn't watch it, Jilly thought, the renovation of Truelove House was going to break her heart.

4

"WOULD YOU LIKE SOME crudités with walnut pesto, sir?" the waiter asked. "Some goat cheese crostini? Or one of these marinated prawns? They're very good."

"I don't think so," Kit said, looking glumly at the elaborate silver tray of hors d'oeuvres the man was carrying. "I was sort of in the mood for anchovy pizza."

"I'm sorry, sir. We seem to have neglected to put that on the menu," the waiter said snootily, gliding away.

"Too bad. I guess that means that curly fries are out of the question, too," Kit said to his departing back.

It was Friday night at twilight, and Kit was doing what he almost always did on Friday nights at twilight: attending somebody-or-other's fancy party, dinner or reception. Tonight, he was at a cocktail party at the home of his clients, Larry and Muffet Cole. Their apartment was on the thirtieth floor of a luxury building overlooking the marina at Biscayne Bay. The building was only five years old, but the Coles had decorated their apartment like an old English manor house, with damask couches, velvet curtains and enough silk braid to rope and tie the entire United States senate.

I don't care if they shipped it over straight from Buckingham Palace, Kit thought, looking around him. *It's stupid.*

Since his return from Key West two days before, Kit had felt odd. For the first time in years, he'd found himself remembering the months he'd spent on the beaches of California, the year he'd turned twenty-five. Something about Jilly Sanderson and Key West had made him once again crave the easy companionship of his early days there, the lazy laughter, the days spent on the beach, even the sloppy spicy foods he'd loved back then. Nachos. Tacos. Pizza. He hadn't had pizza in years, but suddenly he longed for it.

As if that wasn't bad enough, he'd suddenly started to notice interior design...and most of what he noticed annoyed him. The Coles' apartment seemed claustrophobic and pretentious. His own sleek high-tech office seemed sterile and cold. His expensively decorated penthouse apartment was the worst of all. It was like a stage set in an empty theater: beautiful but dead. He had bought himself the perfect life-style, built himself the perfect apartment, he brooded. So why did he suddenly feel like he'd never managed to do any living there?

It's not just the Coles'. My place is stupid, too, he concluded.

Unbidden, Kit's mind filled with pictures of what his apartment would be like with Jilly Sanderson in it. Her dopey so-called antiques warming up his severe modern furniture. Her prissy English teas in the cupboards of his stark kitchen. Her pink volleyball shirt tossed on his bedroom floor. Her slender, sweaty, sweetly excited body twisting beneath him in bed. The images were incredibly arousing. They made the breath catch in his lungs.

Lifting a flute of champagne off a passing waiter's tray, Kit noticed Hank Weinstein staring reprovingly at him from across the crowded room. Kit made a sheepish face back. As Hank was wordlessly reminding him, the room was full of contacts to be made, clients to be charmed, accounts to be won. Besides, all this fantasy was getting him nowhere. Kit had no illusion about his power to alter Jilly's dislike of him. The problem of Brandy might not exist, but all the other obstacles to a relationship between them still

did. Jilly Sanderson probably wanted to drop her volleyball shirt on his bedroom floor about as much as she
wanted to get mugged.

Swallowing a mouthful of champagne, he applied himself to his work. He reassured three clients about the glowing future of Allied shares. He exchanged witty small talk
with a financial reporter from the *Miami Herald*. He even
checked out the women in the room, trying to convince
himself he wasn't just going through the motions. A half
hour later, he noticed that the crowd around Larry and
Muffet Cole had finally thinned, and he headed across the
room to greet them.

"Larry. Muffet. Lovely party," he said, flashing them a
big smile to cover up the empty words.

"Kit, how nice to see you. You haven't been here since
the decorators finished, have you?" Muffet Cole purred,
holding out a tanned long-taloned hand.

"No. It looks great," Kit lied again. *Lord,* he thought, *this
is stupid.*

"Glad you could come, Malone. We've been anxious for
you to meet our daughter," Larry Cole chimed in. "She's
just back from two years of finishing school in Switzer-
land. Brandy, darling, say hello to Christopher Malone."

Brandy smiled and said hello. She was about twenty-
three, with a great set of you-know-whats.

Startled, Kit tried to choke back a laugh. What came out
instead was a snort. Feeling his face redden, he breathed
in, accidentally inhaling his half-swallowed champagne.
Then the partly suppressed laugh got the better of him.
Breathless and choking, he sent a fine spray of liquid onto
Brandy's nubile cleavage.

Larry Cole turned on him, eyes popping behind his
thick glasses. Muffet Cole dabbed furiously at her daughter's chest with a cocktail napkin while Brandy made

whimpering cries of fury. She sounded like an outraged chipmunk. A good finishing school should have cured her of sounding so nasal, Kit thought. He choked again, convulsively, and flapped his arm in halfhearted apology. Neither Muffet nor Larry Cole seemed placated in the least. Brandy kept whimpering. To Kit's undying gratitude, Henry Weinstein magically appeared at his side. *Good old Hank*, Kit thought, gasping for air, *always there when you need him.* Hank mouthed polite words of regret and pulled Kit away, dragging him onto the empty balcony that opened out from the living room's endless expanse.

Unceremoniously Hank shoved Kit into one of the wrought iron metal chairs that dotted the balcony. "Sit," he barked. "Stay. Do not move. If you move, I'll kill you."

A few minutes later, Hank returned with two tall glasses.

"Gin and tonic?" Kit asked tentatively.

"Arsenic on the rocks," Hank said. "You *spat* on a client."

"I just spat on Brandy. It's her parents who are clients," Kit said reasonably, letting the cold liquid trickle down his aching throat.

"Brandy has a two-million-dollar personal trust fund, which you buy the stocks for. Shows how much you know. Shut up for a minute. I'm really mad," Hank said, thin lipped.

Kit propped his crossed ankles on the balcony rail and balanced his knobby metal chair on its back legs. The two men looked silently at the spectacular South Beach skyline. Twilight fell. The lights of the marina glittered against the silvery sky. It was one of the most beautiful views in the world, Kit had always thought. He looked at it now and felt nothing.

It's stupid, too, he thought. *It's all stupid.*

"Daddy?" he said after a decent interval had passed. "I'm really, really sorry. I'll never do it again, I promise. Can I come out of time-out now?"

Hank pulled his chair around to look at Kit. "The only reason we're still here is that the Coles are too embarrassed to have us ushered out by armed security guards," he said. "What got into you?"

"I would explain it, Hank, but it's too long and complicated. I'm really sorry. Trust me, I am. Let's just say it's sort of an inside joke between Jilly and me."

Jilly would appreciate it, Kit thought. *Maybe it lost us a client, but Jilly wouldn't care. Jilly has her priorities straight. Jilly would hate this apartment, and Jilly would laugh.*

Hank closed his eyes. His voice squeaked. "Jilly? Who the hell is Jilly?"

"The co-owner of Lavinia's inn." Kit took another swallow of his drink. His throat was sore, but suddenly he felt good. "The Key West antique dealer. Jeez, Hank, I've been talking about her constantly."

"You haven't said a word."

"I haven't?" Kit asked. "Really? I'm sure I have."

"Not a word," Hank repeated. "I wanted to ask how your date went, in fact, but I hated to ruin your perfect self-absorption with petty chatter."

"Oh," Kit replied, smiling at the memory. Yup, he felt good. Very good. His life might seem stupid, but Jilly definitely didn't. Maybe her dislike of him wasn't such an obstacle after all. "The date. The date was lousy. Well, the end of it was lousy. Not the whole end, just the very end of the end. That was really terrible. But Jilly, Jilly herself... Jilly is...cute."

"Cute," Hank said.

"Yeah. Cute," Kit said dreamily. "She kind of looks...like her cat."

"Like her cat." Henry Weinstein blinked his eyes.

"Yeah," Kit said. "Kind of...tawny...and sleek...and she gets all ruffled up and hissy when she's mad. What are you looking at me like that for? What do you want me to say?"

"Malone," Hank said. "This woman has trashed one of our best accounts and ruined one of the finest financial minds south of the Mason-Dixon line. I expect to hear that she has Greta Garbo's face or Sophia Loren's knockers. Instead you tell me that she's cute, like only 98 percent of the women in America, and that she bears a close resemblance to her cat, Poochie Poo."

"Her cat's name is not Poochie Poo. Her cat's name is Pankhurst. Named after some famous fire-eating feminists," Kit grinned, lacing his fingers behind his head and staring up at the stars. Nah, he didn't just feel good. He had no idea why, except for the fact that Jilly Sanderson existed in the world, but he suddenly felt really, really great.

Hank looked at his friend, his annoyance changing to wonder. "You hate cats. Feminists aren't exactly your best subject, either. This is serious, isn't it, amigo?"

"Mmm. Serious contempt on her side," Kit said. "Serious... Nah. Can't be. It's just infatuation, I figure. A week of looking at her without makeup should cure me. Except that she doesn't really need much makeup. Don't be mad, but I just this minute realized that I need to go down there. To Key West. Just to kind of...get a handle on this. Take charge. A week or so and I'll definitely have it all under control."

"Sure. In one day, she got you so rattled you're spitting on people. In a week, you'll be in a coma."

"I'm happy, Hank," Kit said seriously. "I realize it's ridiculous and pathetic, but be happy for me, anyway."

"I am happy, kid. Really. Congratulations. You're closer to becoming a human being than I've ever seen you. Not a particularly competent human being, but a human being nonetheless." Hank sighed, jiggling the ice cubes in his empty tumbler. "But I would like to point out that this is typical. There are about a million women in Miami and you've dated at least half of them. Why do you have to meet the woman of your dreams in a remote provincial outpost? Or at least, why can't you invite her to Miami and show her the town here?"

"You are radically underestimating this woman's dislike for me. She wouldn't cross the street to save me from dying, much less come to Miami for a date. That's the whole point of going to Key West. She may not be willing to have dinner with me again, but she can't stop me pruning roses on my own property."

"You're going to prune roses?" Hank asked, his eyebrows lifting again.

"Figure of speech. Don't be picky," Kit said.

"Will these all-important Key West roses, not to mention the adorably kittenish Jilly Whatshername, leave you any time to think about trivia like our five gazillion dollars of worthless Allied stock?"

"Yeah. Sure. I can bring a laptop, and hook up to the market. I'm happy to work. I just need to do it from there," Kit said. "Look, I'm really sorry. I know you like me to be in the office."

"Not anymore," Hank said briskly. "Your mind isn't in the office, so it doesn't really matter where your body is."

"Is my...lack of focus that noticeable?" Kit frowned.

"Totally. And that was before the spitting part. Last

Tuesday you were talking about home runs. Today I'd be lucky to get a pop foul out of you."

"Yeah. I'm just not very motivated, suddenly."

"So go to Key West and see this Jilly. When are you going to leave?"

"I thought I'd drive down tonight," Kit said.

"I'm not sure I'd drop in on a woman who hated me at ten o'clock on a Friday evening," Hank answered. "I mean, I don't want to tell you what to do, just because I'm a sane almost-married person and you're a superficial sexist wild man with less capacity for intimacy than a fish stick. But it kind of sets the wrong tone."

"I'm not going to drop in on her, Hank." Kit stood up, stretching. "I just thought it would be nice to sleep in the same town."

Hank shook his head, smiling. He stood up, too, peering through the glass doors into the Cole penthouse. "Pal," he said, "this is not infatuation. This is serious. Kit the ladykiller is gone. Over. History."

"You forget, Hank. This babe hates me. And she's a very intense woman. When Jilly Sanderson hates someone, they probably stay hated for a long time."

"That's like saying she hates earthquakes, or brushfires, or tidal waves. It doesn't matter what she thinks. You're not a person, you're a force of nature." Hank ushered Kit quickly through the apartment and out into the empty hallway before the Coles could notice their departure. "She doesn't have a chance. Maybe I should call and warn her," Hank said as they stepped into the lobby. "Tell her that she's history, too."

"Give her my love. Tell her I'll be there soon. And don't forget to say hi to her famous feminist cat," Kit said, grinning, heading toward his car.

"ALL RIGHT, THEN," Margaret Greer said, picking up the top folder from the neat pile of paperwork on her desk. "The Wilsons, Stefanskis and Ryders are going to the Palms, Patricia Howard is moving to Eden House, the DiSalvos are going to the Conch House and I've put Mr. and Mrs. Locke in the Authors of Key West Guesthouse. They should like it there, they always have a book in their hands and I'm convinced they're bohemians at heart. All of the inn's other reservations for the next three weeks have been changed or transferred. As of right now, what is it, six o'clock on Friday, Truelove House is empty and ready to redecorate." She handed Jilly the folder. "This has all of the change-of-reservation information, plus alarm codes and plumbers' names and other boring but possibly useful information. You can always call me at the Green Mountain Inn, if you need anything." Margaret reached over and switched off the lamp on her desk. "Are you really sure you want to stay here in the inn while I'm gone?"

"Really sure," Jilly said. "I need to get in as much work as I can in the evenings. After all, I'm still finishing the DuMaurier house and supervising my shop during the days. Besides, I want to immerse myself in Truelove House. Commune with Lavinia and the past."

"If you say so. But you might feel a little lonely, all those rooms and no one in them. You could give Kit Malone a call. Maybe he wants to come on down and keep you company."

"Sure. Or I could phone Saddam Hussein. Maybe he wants to come on down and invade Key Largo. That would be fun, too."

"Methinks the lady doth protest too much," Margaret remarked dryly, standing up.

Jilly made a face at her. "Methinks the hotel manager

should keepeth her big nose out of the antique dealer's business," she said.

"You're right," Margaret conceded. "The fact that you're choosing to ignore the exact excitement you were begging your damn cat for is no problem of mine. I'm perfectly happy to fly off to the cool breezes of Vermont and leave you to your own very boring devices. But tell me this, just to humor me."

"What?" Jilly said.

"Don't you find Kit Malone just a little bit attractive?"

"Handsome? Yes. Attractive, as in the sight of him makes me weak in the knees? No. Not at all."

"I don't mind liars. It's bad liars I can't stand," Margaret said reflectively. "Could you grab one of the suitcases? The limo I hired to take me to the airport should be here any minute."

"What's in this thing?" Jilly asked, dragging one of Margaret's suitcases down Truelove House's front hall. "Gold ingots?"

"Clothes. Makeup. Jewelry," Margaret said. "You never know, I might meet a kind and eligible widower while I'm away. Someone to console me in my dotage."

"Oh," Jilly said, dropping the bag at the curb. The two women stood by the gate in the slanted early evening sun. "You're nowhere near your dotage. And I didn't know you were looking."

"I'm not. Unlike you, I'm just not looking away." Margaret put down her handbag and overnight case and wiped her forehead. "Lord, it's hot. I can't wait to hit that cold mountain air. Oh, by the way. When you do talk to Kit, remind him that he promised to explain Lotus 1-2-3 to me when I get back."

"No way. If you want to sell your soul to Satan for a computer software lesson, that's your business. But leave me strictly out of it. I don't intend to speak to Mr. Malone at all if I can help it," Jilly said.

A black limousine pulled smoothly up in front of Truelove House. Margaret pointed her suitcases out to the driver, who was young and handsome. He bowed.

"This looks good already," Margaret said contentedly. "Goodbye, child. Don't work too hard."

"Bye, Margaret," Jilly said, opening the passenger door for her friend. "Have a great time. Don't do anything I wouldn't do."

"Jilly, dear," Margaret said affectionately, giving Jilly a kiss on the cheek and angling her ample form into the car, "that would defeat the entire purpose of the trip. After all, you never do anything."

BROTHERLY, KIT THOUGHT, guiding the Jaguar along the deserted curves of Route 1. Brotherly. That was the key. He'd behaved like a selfish macho maniac around Jilly. First he'd acted like some kind of Miami Beach Scrooge, then he'd turned into Don Juan. Not to mention that idiotic lie about Brandy. No wonder she was resentful and confused.

Well, he decided as the car idled at a Key Largo stoplight, that was going to change. He would be consistent. Helpful. Calm. Well, maybe not calm—that would be asking too much. But helpful, sure. He would help with the renovation, cheerfully, in the spirit Lavinia had planned it. He would be respectful about Key West and nice to Jilly's friends. He wouldn't keep staring at her trying to figure out if she had on any underwear. He'd wait for her to make a move on him. Until then, he'd be innocent as an angel. Well, maybe not an angel, either. But brotherly. Definitely brotherly. Even if it killed him. Which, come to think of it, it definitely might.

JILLY TURNED OFF THE faucet and leaned back in the deep claw-footed bathtub. Underneath the froth of rose-scented bubbles, the water was almost painfully hot. She adjusted her neck so that it rested comfortably on the cool curve of the tub and sighed with pleasure. After Margaret's departure, Jilly had used the evening to start her detailed inventory of the inn. She now had twenty pages of notes, hundreds of ideas and an aching back. She was dusty, exhausted and content.

Aimlessly stirring the bubbly water with her hand, she looked around the old bathroom. Despite her fatigue, she felt the usual tingle of excitement at beginning a decorating project. As she'd said to Kit Malone, the inn was in basically good shape, the plumbing and electricity fine, much of the furniture attractive and sturdy. All she had to do was give new life to what was there. Refresh the old paint, polish the furniture and brass fixtures, sand and refinish the scuffed floors, choose new fabrics and rugs. Then just pick small accessories that would make the inn a charming, comfortable home away from home.

Washing herself with a bar of rose-scented soap, Jilly thought about the past few days. Kit Malone had been true to his original plan. He had left Jilly, the inn and Key West strictly alone. Their intimate dinner, their various moments of truth, their passionate kiss—it might as well never have happened.

Jilly wanted to feel grateful. He could only disrupt things, and she already felt disrupted enough. But somehow his silence wasn't as calming as she wanted it to be. Even with the renovation to think about, the nagging discontent she'd felt before finding out about Lavinia's will had only grown stronger in the four days since she'd met Kit. Not, of course, that Kit Malone was the solution. Excitement was one thing, and Kit was another. He was like a hurricane or an avalanche, she thought ruefully, scrubbing her back with a long-handled wooden brush. Once the drama was over, he would leave nothing but wreckage in his wake.

Eventually, of course, the renovation and the running of the inn would force her to deal with him. They would chat, or write, or fax. Professional, she thought. Simply, coolly professional. She wouldn't insult his suit. He wouldn't call her gorgeous. They would definitely not kiss. She would be objective. She wouldn't flare into anger or burst into tears. She would be cool, calm. Well, maybe not calm. That was asking too much. But professional. That was the key.

Clean and drowsy, Jilly toweled herself dry and wrapped herself in an old silk dressing gown, lovingly chosen from one of Key West's vintage clothing stores. Slowly she padded through the inn, locked the front door, set the burglar alarm and left a small lamp burning in the hall. Over the hall table hung a portrait of Lavinia and Sam. Jilly stood, looking up at their smiling faces. Lavinia had been more than a friend, she thought fondly. She had been the wise and funny mother Jilly had never had. How wonderful it was to have this chance to honor her memory. *Don't worry, Lavinia,* Jilly thought fondly. *I'll do a good job, with your darned grandson or without him.*

Jilly climbed the front staircase and headed toward the bedroom she was using. She pulled on the big white T-shirt she slept in and slipped between the sheets. It was time to get some sleep.

A sound woke her at midnight. An odd, suspicious sound. The Key West night was full of rustling leaves, cooing birds, yelling tourists. But this was a sneaky, surreptitious noise, somewhere close. Jilly held her breath and listened hard. Not outside, she thought. Somewhere inside. Downstairs.

A quiet but confident series of footsteps, in fact, wandering through the first-floor rooms. The soft clink and thump of objects being lifted. A low cough. Jilly's heart thundered. Carefully she slid out of bed. She used the room telephone to make a quick whispered call to the police, then listened again. By now the footsteps were louder, closer to the stairs.

Silently Jilly pulled open her bedroom door and tiptoed into the hallway. Pulling the closest thing she had to a weapon from a pile of odds and ends she'd stashed in a corner, she padded soundlessly to the edge of the stairs. She knew she should probably just hide until the police came, but the thought of Lavinia's things being pilfered made her furious. Besides, it sounded like the intruder was heading for the stairs. She had nothing to lose.

Wiping her wet hands on her T-shirt, she willed herself to keep her voice calm. "I have a gun pointed at your head, and I'm going to blow you away if you move one step farther," she said loudly. She was pleased with how commanding she sounded. There was a quick movement from below. "I mean it," she asserted. "I've already called 911. The police are going to drive up any minute."

"Jilly?" a deep voice said from downstairs.

"Who's that? Don't move!" Jilly yelled in confusion.

"Jilly? Jilly, it's okay. It's Kit. Kit—Christopher—Malone. I didn't know anyone was staying here. Margaret told me the inn was empty. Jilly, don't panic. I'm just going to move far enough forward that you can see that it's me. Don't shoot me, okay? Good girl."

Jilly watched Kit's unmistakable head emerge into the lamplit hallway. Relief made her sag against the banister. Then panic turned to fury. "How dare you?" she spat. "Do you have any idea how terrified I was? How dare you walk into my house and scare the hell out of me like this?"

"It's not your house, exactly," Kit answered absently, looking up at her as he took the stairs two at a time. Her golden brown hair was wildly tousled and her face was white. Under her huge and baggy T-shirt, which came down almost to her knees, she was shaking like a leaf.

"Jilly," he said, standing in front of her, "I'm truly sorry. I really had no idea you'd be here." He looked down at the object she clutched in her hand, distracted. "What the hell is that?" he rumbled.

"A shelf bracket," Jilly muttered.

"A *shelf bracket*? You sashayed out to confront an intruder with a *shelf bracket*? That is really stupid. Where's the gun?" Relief and a quick, crazy, protective anger made Kit's voice rough.

"There is no gun! I would never, under any circumstances, ever own a gun! But I was so scared, and I couldn't figure out how anyone could get past the alarm, and I knew the police wouldn't get here before you'd stolen Lavinia's things. I didn't know what to do!" Jilly glared up at him, shaking furiously. "And now you're yelling at me! As usual!"

"Oh, damn," Kit said under his breath. All of his indignation dissolved in the face of Jilly's vulnerability. He felt a rush of tenderness for her, a feeling warmer and more urgent than anything he'd ever felt before. He watched as her eyes filled with tears. Gently he gathered her into his arms. After a moment's resistance, she let herself be held.

She was so delicate, and warm from sleep, and she smelled like talcum powder. She was the perfect height, just tall enough for him to cradle her cheek against the angle of his neck and shoulder. He could feel her small high breasts and slim hips as he rocked her but he ignored their arousing softness, concerned only with giving her comfort.

"All right, sweetheart," he murmured into her hair.

"You're safe, everything's okay, there aren't any more thoughtless fools blundering in to terrify you. No more—" He couldn't suppress the smallest of smiles, which he smothered into her hair, "no more need to fend off homicidal burglars with minor domestic hardware. It's all right, just go ahead and let it out." And Jilly did. Comforted by the strong warmth of his arms and by the gentle rocking motion of his body as he held her, she abandoned herself to tears.

Fifteen minutes later the police had been sent away and a big pot of Earl Grey tea stood on the inn's oval dining table. Jilly's legs still trembled, but her heart no longer raced. She felt sheepish about her outburst. God, she'd been practically plastered against him. Not to mention the fact that even in her distress, being plastered against him had felt great. He was big enough to make her feel cherished and feminine, and he smelled wonderful and masculine, and he'd been so warm, so reassuring, so tender. Of course, she had made a fool out of herself by bursting into tears. And she must look terrible. He probably thought she was an idiot. And not an especially pretty idiot at that.

Not that she cared, of course.

Embarrassed, she returned to practical problems.

"So," she said. "What in the world are you doing here?"

"I decided you were right," Kit said mildly, pouring her another cup of tea. "This is a special project. We should both be part of it. I'm going to hook up the computer so that I can watch the market in the mornings, and I'm going to help out with the renovation in the afternoons."

"Am I supposed to be touched?" Jilly said waspishly, touched.

"Nah," Kit said. "No one who knows you would expect you to feel such a boring little emotion, babe."

"Malone, if you start calling me 'babe,'" Jilly said, glaring at him, "I'm going to take this shelf bracket and shove it—"

"Jillian Mabel!" Kit threw up his hands in mock horror. "Really, how vulgar. It must be the shock speaking. You're tense and cold." He looked at her, focusing. "Right. You're tense and cold. Let me get you a blanket, or your bathrobe, or something."

"My robe is on the chair in the bedroom I'm using, at the top of the stairs," Jilly said. Belatedly aware of her half nakedness, she crossed her arms over her chest. For good measure, she crossed her legs as well. The hem of her sleep shirt rode up her thigh and she tugged it down. "I would get it myself, but I'm scared that someone would leap out at me from the darkness."

"Don't worry, ba— I mean Jilly. The inn is lit up like a Christmas tree. I don't think we're going to get burgled tonight," Kit said, trying to ignore both her enticingly long tanned thighs and the by-now-familiar question of whether she was wearing underwear. Sometime when he and this innocent little nitwit were actually speaking to each other, he was going to explain to her the effect her loose clothes and nice body had on a man. But not anytime soon. Right now he was being brotherly.

"I wasn't worried about burglars," Jilly said crossly to his departing back, tugging her T-shirt down again. "They would be no problem. I was worried about hateful people from what I hoped was my past dropping in. If you're here, anyone could follow. For all I know, my mother, or my ex-husband, Claude, or Billy McIntyre could be all ready to leap in through a window."

Kit's head reemerged around the door lintel. "Who's Billy McIntyre?"

"You remind me of him. A lot. Never mind," Jilly said wearily. "Get upstairs already."

"Here's your robe," Kit said cheerfully, handing her the old silk dressing gown a few minutes later. "Either yours or Clark Gable's. And I found a great room for myself. That small blue one at the end of the hallway."

"You're staying here?" Jilly said, looking up from the sash of her robe in shock.

"Of course. Where else would I stay?"

The Hong Kong Hilton is just about perfect, Jilly thought. "I don't know. The possibility just hadn't occurred to me."

"Obviously, it makes sense for me to stay here. Plus, I can protect you against intruders. I don't like the idea of you rattling around this place alone at night."

"I don't like the idea of the two of us rattling around this place," Jilly objected, disconcerted. *Particularly not at night.* "What will people think?"

Kit grinned. "This isn't 1810, goofball. Two unmarried people staying in an empty hotel will barely rate a yawn. Besides, Sanderson, I can assure you that your virtue is utterly safe with me."

"That isn't what I meant, Malone," Jilly said, gritting her teeth.

"Completely, totally safe," Kit said, ignoring her. "Don't get me wrong, Jilly. You're really cute. But somehow I'm going to manage to stop myself from sneaking down the hall and ravishing you. It'll be tough, but I promise." *But only because in a week or so you're going to be sneaking down the hall and ravishing me.*

"I am not afraid of being ravished, Malone. Stop twisting my words. If one thing is clear, it's that I am not your type," Jilly said, stung. If there was one thing she didn't need to hear right now, it was how resistible she was to Kit Malone. "I never have been your type. I never will be your type. I would be at greater risk with the Pope. I understand. Okay?" Standing up, she started to stack their teacups and saucers. "Let me explain my feelings more clearly. I do not want you here. I don't want your company, much less your body. I want to have the inn all to myself. Me and Lavinia. With no help from you or anyone else."

"Well, that's too bad," Kit said briskly. "It's half my property, and she was my grandmother, and I'm staying." He looked shrewdly at her stubborn face. "You can always go home, of course. Unlike me, you have a perfectly comfortable house here. But I wouldn't have taken you for a coward, Sanderson."

"I'm not afraid of you, Malone. Don't be ridiculous." Jilly cast about for a way out of this absurd situation. If she moved back home she would look like she was scared, and she'd feel like an idiot in front of Margaret, too. Besides, she wanted to be in Truelove House, Kit Malone or no Kit Malone. "And anyway, the roof of my house is being repaired," she added untruthfully, making a mental note to call the roof repair people in the morning. "I have no choice but to stay here. I suppose we can make it work. It's a big place. We barely have to see each other."

"Fine," Kit said, calmly.

"Fine," Jilly repeated, with an equal lack of expression. "Well, then. I think I'll go to bed."

"Fine," Kit said again. "Uh, Jilly?"

"What?" Jilly said from the door.

"You don't need a weapon. I'll protect you. You can leave the shelf bracket here."

"Gee, thanks, Malone," Jilly called sarcastically over her shoulder. "You're so helpful. It's going to be so nice to have a man around the house."

"You bet it will," Kit said to himself.

"WHAT'S THE CAPITAL of Texas?"

"Austin," Kit answered, dropping into one of the

wrought iron chairs that dotted the inn's terrace. It was a gloriously clear and breezy Key West morning. He'd been right when he'd talked to Hank last night. It had felt good to sleep in the same town with Jilly Sanderson. "Why?"

Jilly kept her nose in the paper. It felt weird having him here, knowing he'd slept and showered and dressed in those tight, tattered blue jeans only a few yards from her bedroom. "Crossword," she said gruffly, scribbling a word in pen. "There's coffee, and croissants in the basket."

"Thanks," Kit said, grinning at the top of her head. As he poured his coffee and buttered his croissant he made a quick surreptitious survey. Jilly was wearing baggy white shorts, which bared a nice length of tanned thigh, and an even baggier white T-shirt, which she'd tied in a knot at her hip. Her skin was fresh and dewy, devoid of makeup, and her shining hair was in tumbled disarray. As usual, her feet were bare. She was studying her crossword with the same intense concentration Michelangelo probably gave to the Sistine ceiling. *Shy*, Kit thought.

Or mad. Knowing Jilly, probably mad.

God, she was cute, even in the morning.

"There wouldn't happen to be any bacon or eggs or cereal, would there?" he asked. That would get her attention.

Her head emerged from the paper. She stared at him, raising her eyebrows. "What happened? Did someone elect me Queen of the Larder while I was asleep?" she said sarcastically.

"It was just a question," he said.

"If it was just a question," Jilly retorted, "the question should have been, 'Hey, Jilly, I practically gave you a coronary last night, and I'm screwing up your life again today, so I'm going to be a pal and cook up some eggs this morning. Do you want some?'"

"Okay. Do you?"

"No. Seriously, Malone. If you want to stay for a week, stay for a week. It's your life. Just don't look to me for meals."

"Seriously, Sanderson, it's not a problem. We can take turns at cooking dinner, unless one of us is out. We'll be on our own for breakfast and lunch, unless one of us happens to cook up some eggs or something. I also plan to do my own laundry, make my own bed and generally handle my own needs." *Well, most of them. There are a few you could help me with.* "And I'm happy to search the larder on my own. Only, what's a larder?"

"The kitchen," Jilly said, ignoring his teasing lazy eyes and dazzling smile by sticking her head back into her paper, "is at the back of the house, all the way down the corridor. I'll give you a hint—when you trip over the stove, you're in the right room. However, there are no eggs or bacon in it."

"There will be soon," Kit said playfully. "You need a man's fuel to do a man's work."

"Famed Zulu king. Five letters. Man's work? What are you going to do, invade Grenada? Exactly what man's work do you plan to do this week?"

"Chaka. The Zulu king, that is. As for me, I'm going to help with any guy things that arise. Move furniture. Update the computer system. Relandscape the garden."

"The garden?" Jilly lifted her head and threw him a skeptical look. "Suddenly you're a plant expert? I bet you've never done gardening in your life."

"I got a gold star for my zinnias in Mrs. Herbert's first grade class, and I have a very good relationship with Mattie the office plant lady. I can learn."

"Right. You might want to start on something smaller

than the grounds of a hotel. How about I buy you a cactus?"

"Jilly," Kit said, patiently, waving at the beds behind the terrace, "what do you notice when you look around? Plants, right? Growing plants. Too many growing plants, in fact. We are not talking about trying to plant orchids on the moon. This is mostly going to be a matter of cutting back, of making a few small changes here and there. I will get expert advice. I will go slowly. I know you have a proprietary interest in this place, but don't worry."

"I'm not worried, Malone," Jilly said. But she was. There was no telling what a man this aggressive could do with a pair of pruning shears in his hand. In three days the lush garden would probably look like a putting green.

"Yes, you are. Well, worry about your half of the project."

"Fine. I will." Jilly bent her head to the puzzle again. A moment later, she raised it again. "Nobel literature prize-winner? Six letters?"

"Neruda. Maybe," Kit said.

"Thanks. How do you know these things?"

"I may be a cretin," Kit answered, "but I'm a cretin who knows his current events."

"I'm not worrying, mind you," Jilly continued as if he hadn't spoken. "I'm just curious. I don't understand why you want to mess around with the landscaping."

"I told you. I want to be part of this project, and I don't want to interfere with what you're doing inside the inn. Besides, I have an idea about this garden." *An idea that has to do with exploring the question of your lack of underwear under the palmetto fronds. An idea about which you do not want to know. Not yet, at least.* "A vision, you might say. Let me have my fun." Kit picked up his coffee cup and the empty croissant basket. "I'm going to bring this stuff to the kitchen and check the contents of the—what do you call it?—larder. If you want some of the dinner I'm cooking, be here at seven. Now, before I go uproot some mighty oaks with my bare hands, are there any other clues you need help with?"

"Yes. Three-letter word for uninvited nuisance, beginning with *K*."

"God, Jilly, you're so cute in the morning," Kit said sincerely, patting her head as he left.

5

THE PHONE RANG WHILE Jilly was stenciling one of the small bathrooms. Cursing under her breath, she dabbed a final bit of pigment into place, climbed down the rickety ladder, and crossed the room. She picked up the receiver with a blue-spattered hand.

"Hey, Jilly girl," Ned Winston's cheerful voice boomed. "How are ya?"

"Fine, Ned," Jilly smiled. "The inn is looking great. All the work you guys did last weekend really made a difference."

"Great. Any time, kiddo. You know that. Our muscles are your muscles," Ned said. "Listen. Is Killer there?"

Jilly stared at the receiver in disbelief. "Killer?" she said incredulously. "Who's that, one of the Seven Evil Dwarfs? I'm sorry, but there is no Killer in this residence."

"Very funny, babe. Okay. Kit. Christopher. Mr. Malone. Master. Whatever you call him. Is he there? He wanted help with the sprinkler system and I've got some time right now, if he wants to do it."

"I'll get him." Jilly put the receiver down and headed downstairs, rolling her eyes.

Congratulations, Jilly, she thought sourly. *You've been outnumbered.*

Ever since Kit's dramatic return to Key West two weeks before, life in Truelove House had dramatically changed. So much for quiet solitary evenings communing with La-

vinia and the past. Now it was like living in Boystown.
Testosterone West. The Y-Chromosome Hotel.

Not only had Kit attached himself to the place like a bar-
nacle, but the men of the Conch Team had attached themselves along with him. The good news was that Ned, Jeff
and Larry were helping with the renovation. Cheerfully,
as though summoned by some mysteriously silent male
call, they stripped paint, wielded sanding machines and
carted debris.

The bad news was that Jilly felt like a cat at a dog con-
vention. She was the single fifth wheel in a veritable orgy
of male bonding. Jeff, Larry, Ned and Kit played volleyball
together, went fishing together, drank beer together. They
always invited her to come along, and sometimes she did.
But she could only take so much. It was enough to make
any self-respecting feminist sick.

It was almost bad enough to make her wish for the old
efficient, snobbish, utterly unfriendly Kit Malone back.

Jilly peered out the inn's back door. Kit had been working on relandscaping the yard around the inn with typical
Malone obsessiveness. As always, he was there, digging
up something that looked like the plant from *The Little
Shop of Horrors*. As always, he was wearing nothing but an-
cient tennis shoes, a pair of filthy jeans and blindingly
white briefs. She knew about the briefs because a sliver of
waistband showed when the jeans slipped a bit down
those narrow hips, which they tended to do a little too often for her comfort.

"Oh, Killer," she called in saccharine tones. "Killer,
dearest, can you spare a moment? Your little friend Ned's
on the phone."

Kit looked back over his shoulder, grinning. "Hang on."
He wiped his hands on the back of his jeans and ambled
toward the stoop on which she stood.

"Do I detect a hint of possessiveness in your voice, Sanderson? Feeling a bit miffed that your beloved Conch Team actually likes me?" he asked, glancing down at her face as he walked indoors by her side.

"Don't be ridiculous, Malone," she said, dropping into a chair. "I've got more important things on my mind than your current rankings in the Key West popularity polls." His question hit home, though. She didn't feel jealous, exactly. She just wasn't sure she was ready for Kit Malone to become such a fixture in her life. What was going to happen when he skipped on back to Miami? The last thing she was going to need then would be Larry, Jeff and Ned asking her where he was. "You can bond as much as you want together," she said. "Do whatever it is boys do."

Kit laughed down at her, his gray eyes twinkling. How was it that she'd ever thought they were cold eyes? Conceited, yes. Irritating, yes. But not cold. "Oh, you know what we do. Kill bunnies. Burp. Compare cars. Bet on meaningless things like the number of fives on a dollar bill. Make women miserable. Nothing fancy."

"Go for it," Jilly said, raising her chin condescendingly.

The new angle of her head placed his expanse of flat, muscular, tanned belly right in her line of vision. She looked hastily away.

"Thanks for your permission, Sanderson," Kit said, balancing the phone receiver against his bare broad shoulder. "Ned? Kit. Sanderson here has just given us permission to bond. You ready to go?"

"Up yours, Kit Malone," Jilly said under her breath as she started up the stairs.

Kit's head poked out from around the parlor door frame. "By the way, Jilly," he called, "you have stencil paint on your nose."

"MARGARET!" JILLY CRIED the following Monday, leaning out of the second-floor front bedroom window and waving a paintbrush at her friend. "I missed you! Welcome back!"

Margaret waved and pointed toward the inn. Moments later, the two women met in Margaret's office. Jilly hugged her friend hard, then stepped back to look at her. "You look fantastic," Jilly said. "Vermont agrees with you."

"It was a wonderful vacation," Margaret agreed, smiling.

"Tell me all. Start with the sexy parts, if any."

"I did meet a lovely man," Margaret said cautiously. "Attractive and very attentive. Of course, he lives in Chicago, so we'll just have to see. What about you?"

"Nope. No attentive men from Chicago here," Jilly answered brightly. *Just the lunatic gardener from hell.* Jilly did not look forward to telling Margaret about Kit's surprise sojourn at Truelove House. "But yours is great news. Tell me more."

"I'll give you all the details over dinner tonight if you want. Right now, though, I need to get back to work. How's the inn? And what about the renovation?"

"Everything was fine. No surprises," Jilly said. *Sure. And about that bridge I was going to sell you...* "And the renovation is going fine. You can't see much, but progress is definitely being made."

"Speaking of which," Margaret asked, "what in the world is going on in the garden?"

As though on cue, the office door flew open and Kit breezed in, wearing his usual dirt-smeared jeans and brandishing a pair of pruning scissors. "Where the living hell are the lopping shears, Sanderson? How many times do I have to tell you that they're not for bloody wallpaper? Next time you touch them I'm going to—oh, Margaret," he said, surprised. "Sorry, I didn't know you were here. Welcome back."

"Thank you," Margaret said calmly, looking from one to the other, waiting.

Jilly stared at Kit, willing him to answer. To her fury, he just grinned and raised one sharp black eyebrow. "Uh," she said, feeling her cheeks flush. "Margaret. Malone here invited himself to stay with us while he helped out with the renovation. He's in what used to be room Number 6, which is now masquerading as landfill."

"Right, Margaret," Kit said, flashing one of his thousand-watt smiles. "What Jilly is trying to say is that when I'm in the privacy of my room I drop my socks on the floor. A real crime. But perhaps you didn't know that she's this year's Tidy Closet poster child."

"Give me a break," Jilly said, avoiding Kit's ironic eye. To Margaret, she said, "He has a pile of dirty clothes on his floor the size of Gibraltar, some of which probably date from the Civil War. If he ever decides to do his laundry, America might finally locate Jimmy Hoffa."

"Of course," Kit grinned at Margaret, "you might wonder why, if my room bothers her so much, she doesn't just keep her nose out of it."

Jilly lifted her chin, nettled. "On the contrary, Margaret, you'll understand that those of us who are working inside all day might be troubled by the condition of the rooms, while those who slop away outside never notice. Oh, that's right. Kit has decided to fix the garden. That's why it's looking so bare—he's Miami's answer to Agent Orange. You might do me a favor and try to convince him that plumbago would be perfect in front of the porch. I've tried to explain, but he's having trouble grasping the concept."

"Don't worry, Margaret, no need to waste your breath," Kit replied, irritated, "since any moron with even a rudimentary knowledge of plants understands that plumbago needs full sun and the front garden doesn't have it. As long as we're at it, though, you might remind our lovely little decorator that this is a hotel, not a private home. Half of these fancy little knickknacks she's buying are going to end up visiting Peoria in somebody's suitcase."

Jilly put her hands on her hips. "As Margaret will tell you, Mr. Cynic, Truelove House guests do not steal things."

Kit leaned back against Margaret's desk, crossed his arms on his chest and fixed her with a cool gray stare. "As Margaret will tell *you*, Miss Know-it-all, the front of the hotel needs a shade-loving plant."

Margaret banged a stapler on the desk and fixed Kit and Jilly with an icy stare. "Stop it right now, you two," she said. "This is not the United Nations general assembly, and I am not a simultaneous translator. If you wish to communicate with each other, you'll have to do it directly. Not, and I do mean *not*, in my office. In fact, I want both of you out of here right now. I have work to do."

"Margaret—" Kit said.

"But, Margaret," Jilly began.

"Don't Margaret me. I'm not interested. And close the door behind you. If the two of you can agree on how to do it, that is."

Grinning down at Jilly, Kit turned to go. Reluctantly Jilly followed behind him. "The front of the hotel needs something blue, and the plumbago will be perfect," she said, elbowing him in the ribs as they turned into the corridor.

"The guests are gonna steal every damned thing you don't glue down," Kit said, bumping her with his hip.

"Will not," Jilly said.

"Will, too," he answered, heading out the back door.

"Mule-headed cretin," Jilly yelled after him.

"Idealistic fool," Kit called from the garden.

In the office, Margaret Greer turned on her desk light, settled her reading glasses on her nose and smiled. "You know, Lavinia," she said to the air, "this cockamamie scheme of yours might just work after all."

THE DAY AFTER MARGARET'S return, Jilly had dinner with Belle. They sat in the cool back room at Ernest's and chatted lazily about Jilly's shop and Belle's kids.

"So much for exotic experiments in child rearing chez Lincoln," Belle said finally. "Tell me what's happening with you."

"Well, the renovation is going wonderfully," Jilly admitted. "Thanks to your help, and Linc's, and the volleyball guys, of course."

"And thanks to Kit Malone, I presume?" Belle took a sip of her mineral water.

"Kit Malone!" Jilly scowled. "Some big help he is."

"But, Jilly, Ed Parks over at the nursery in Tavernier said that Kit's been working like a fiend at the landscaping."

"Kit Malone," Jilly said darkly, "is working like a fiend all right."

Moodily she toyed with the olives on her appetizer plate. For a day or two there, once she'd gotten used to him, Jilly had actually thought she could get to like Kit's constant presence at Truelove House. He had turned out to be capable, fun and surprisingly easy to be with. In fact, if you ignored the messiness of his room and the obstinacy of his opinions, he had gone out of his way to be the perfect companion. A buddy. A pal. Sort of like the jolly big brother she'd never had.

Perfect. If only she had been able to feel more...sisterly. But when she thought of Kit, it wasn't Kit-the-big-brother that appeared in her mind's eye. The images that popped uninvited into her head were always of a very different and very disturbing Kit: Kit the beautiful, the physical, the sexual male animal.

If she closed her eyes, an image of Kit stretching to install a ceiling fan, his polo shirt riding up to expose a sliver of hard, bare belly danced across her mind. Kit striding out of the surf, black hair and quivering muscles gleaming with saltwater. Kit sprawling on the Victorian sofa in the Truelove House parlor, his casual and lazy male form the perfect contrast to its fussy elegance.

If she closed her eyes tighter, she could hear Kit's laugh, a gloriously deep uninhibited sound. And smell Kit's scent, an intoxicating fragrance that seemed to be compounded of equal parts salt, sweat, sunscreen and garden loam, with a slight overlay of male musk that was uniquely his own.

She could picture Kit's neck, over which his glossy black curls tumbled. Kit's chest, now tanned to a warm brown in the Key West sun, covered with a thoroughly masculine swirl of black hair almost hiding his very sexy nipples. Kit's expressive long-fingered hands. Kit's feet, which were narrow and strong and highly arched.

Jilly had never before felt this kind of physical admiration for a man. It had been Claude's approval she'd desired, not his body. Impatient and critical in bed, he had never made her long for anything more. Now all her buried sexual instincts were making a very unwelcome comeback.

It was humiliating, Jilly thought morosely, to be so enamored of a man that you fantasized about his feet.

Particularly when the man whose feet you dreamed of was perfectly content to see you as a combination of younger sister, little helper and the jolly girl next door.

And when he seemed blissfully unaware that you were a woman and he was a man and the two of you had shared a single very passionate kiss...before, that is, you started living together in a house with thirteen beds.

"Earth to Jilly," Belle called, waving her pink plastic stirrer in front of Jilly's abstracted eyes. "Come on. Out with it."

"You'll just laugh."

"I will not laugh." Belle stretched her arm to spear a bite of Jilly's Dijon chicken. "I didn't laugh when you let Raoul of Key Largo perm your hair. I didn't laugh when Jeff dropped a cherry pie on your white dress at the last volleyball party. I didn't even laugh when I met your excruciatingly pompous ex-husband, though God knows that man's a joke. I am not going to laugh now. Just spit it out, okay?"

Jilly sighed. "I'm very—attracted—to Kit."

"That's your big revelation? Every woman in the Keys is attracted to Kit. What's the big deal?"

"The big deal is that every other woman in the Keys doesn't have to live with him. The big deal is that I don't like being attracted to a man who's not attracted to me."

"And what makes you think he's not attracted to you? Boy, that chicken is good. Can I have another bite?"

"Sure. I'm not hungry. Everything makes me think he's not attracted. He hasn't done a single thing since he's been here to demonstrate the slightest hint of interest."

"Except sit here in Key West for weeks."

"Days. So he's taking a vacation. So what?"

"The guy owns a Jaguar, Jilly. He's a partner in a fancy financial firm. I'm sure he could afford to do something more relaxing than stick plants in the ground, if all he wanted was a vacation."

"Okay, so tell me, then," Jilly said, frustrated. "If he's interested in me, why isn't he doing anything about it?"

Belle reached over and helped herself to the rest of Jilly's vegetables, which Jilly had been pushing morosely around her plate. "Are you sure you haven't missed anything? Some invitation, some little hint? Guys are strange sometimes."

"Kit's strange, all right. But he's done nothing with me he couldn't have done with his first grade teacher. Less." Jilly put down her fork and waved the waitress over to order coffee. "I haven't felt this unattractive since I was married to Claude."

"You have, too. You always feel unattractive—you're probably the most insecure beautiful woman I've ever met, and I've met a few. And besides, unattractiveness is not the problem."

"Claude said it was. For all I know, Kit feels the same."

Belle shook her head in disbelief. "Jilly, you have a brain—use it. Would Claude bring you three bags of manure fertilizer in the back of his expensive sports car, just because it was good for your garden? Would Claude deign to dig a hole in the ground, even if there was buried treasure beneath it? Would Claude have joined the Conch Team—and even if he did, would the guys actually like him? More importantly, could you wave at our waitress again? I'm going to order dessert."

Jilly eyed her friend suspiciously. "Jeez, Belle. Are you pregnant?"

"No. Linc and I do not, I repeat not, want more twins. We're being very careful."

"I hope so. But you're eating like a pregnant lady."

"No way."

"Absolutely, positively, unequivocally no way? Physical evidence and all?"

"No...not exactly. There's a theoretical possibility, I guess. Which I am going to ignore. And don't try to change the subject. Kit is not even a little bit like Claude."

Sighing, Jilly had to surrender. "Well, all right, you win. But even if I concede, for the sake of argument, that Kit is a normal, everyday guy with a trustworthy heart and decent values, who's staying in Key West because he's interested in me—and mind you, I'm not convinced that any of this is actually true—just when is this paragon of restraint going to make some kind of move?"

"I have no idea," Belle said airily. "Why don't you make some kind of move yourself?"

"Because that's his job. And besides, I don't want to humiliate myself, that's why."

"Has anyone ever told you it's not 1955 anymore? You're a disgrace to liberated women everywhere, Sanderson." Suddenly Belle's dancing eyes turned serious. "Do you know what the difference between you and me is?"

"Do I get a magic decoder ring if I'm right? I know! Four babies—six babies—and a man with no hair on his back?" Jilly teased.

"Joke all you want. The difference is that I," Belle said, stabbing the air with her finger for emphasis, "am not afraid of making a fool of myself for love. You are. That's the difference. When it comes to love, you're so afraid of making a mistake that you're paralyzed. Well, if you want to wrap your heart in cotton wool for the rest of your life, that's fine. But you can't do that and figure out Kit Malone at once. You just have to jump in there and make a fool out of yourself like everyone else," Belle finished.

She looked at Jilly's damp and vulnerable eyes. "Oh, honey, don't cry. I know I'm lecturing you, but I'm doing it because I love you."

"I know." Jilly smiled at her friend. The truth was, she

thought, Belle was right. Here she was, living in one of the world's most sensual places, staying in a romantic old inn with a gorgeous if unbelievably opinionated guy who seemed to live for the pleasure of planting her garden. With the wrong plants, but still... Any woman in her right mind would have jumped the guy's bones ten days ago, and damn the consequences."

"I'm not crying because I'm mad at you," Jilly said. "I'm crying because you're right."

"I know that's unusual, but it's not a tragedy," Belle teased gently, trying to lighten their mood. She waved away Jilly's offered cash. "Forget it, kiddo. My treat. I ate all the food, anyway."

"All right. I'm changing. Starting tomorrow," Jilly said, "I am going to charge confidently into the romantic fray. In fact, I need you to go shopping with me. I'm tired of being Kit Malone's cute little tomboy next door. I realize that nakedness is the ultimate goal, but seducing him is still going to require clothes."

"Fine. Tomorrow afternoon, okay?" Belle said, signing the restaurant's charge slip with a flourish.

"You know, I was really just teasing before, about the pregnancy. Do you seriously think there's a chance?" Jilly said as they walked onto Greene Street.

"Maybe. I haven't eaten that much in exactly four years. I'm going to go home and panic."

Jilly gave her friend a hug at the corner. "Hey, what a coincidence. I'm going to go home and panic, too."

"Have a brownie or something while you do it," Belle said practically. "It doesn't take away the terror, but it makes it more fun."

"OKAY, BOYS, CONCENTRATE," Kit said, rapping his beer bottle against the side of the bar to get the Conch Team's attention. "What am I going to do about Jilly?"

"What about Jilly?" Ned asked.

"Nothin' wrong with Jilly," Jeff added.

"Jilly's fine. Jilly's great," Larry said.

It was sunset at Mallory Square. The four men had played a little basketball, then walked over to Jimmy Buffet's Margaritaville Bar. The air was warm, the breeze was cool, the Dos Equis were cold. They had had four beers apiece, more than Kit usually drank in a week. They were all as mellow as they were going to be short of lobotomy. If he was going to get their input on the Jilly problem, it was now or never.

And, boy, did he need help. So far he'd spent ten days in Key West. He'd had more fun and felt more alive than he had in years. He'd been as brotherly as a Boy Scout. Life was great. Except that every single day had been a wasteland of lost opportunities.

There was that first morning, when he hadn't made love to Jilly right there on the terrace in the middle of her damned crossword puzzle. And every meal thereafter.

There was the time he didn't wipe the stencil paint off her adorable nose and just let things develop. The time he glimpsed her bending over to touch up a baseboard and just managed to prevent himself from grabbing her deliciously cute rear. The time when their bodies had collided full force as they both lunged for a Lobster Team volleyball serve. And all those lonely, long nights when he hadn't stomped down the hall from his bedroom to hers and done what would have come very, very naturally.

Kit had always been a hit-and-run kind of guy. If a woman wasn't as willing as he was, he just moved on. Because no matter how attractive a woman seemed to him, it had never really mattered how she felt or what she did or whether she walked away.

But Jilly... Jilly mattered. A lot. He'd seen her without makeup, seen her irritable and shy and fierce and fragile, seen her when her stomach hurt and when a client made her furious and when she decided to argue some perfectly ridiculous point, which she did with unbelievable stubbornness. The more he saw, the more he wanted her. He knew so much about her, but he didn't know what to do. He could tell she was attracted to him, and he could tell that she was scared and vulnerable and resistant. He could try forcing the issue, but that meant taking the risk of seeing her walk away. And the mere thought of her leaving made his gut clench and sweat break out on his forehead.

So he drank more beer than usual to dull the longing. He took cold showers. He threw himself into the orgy of exhausting physical activity that Jilly, in her innocence, denigrated as male bonding. He even decided to turn to these three lovable goons for help.

"That's exactly my point," he said to them now. "Jilly's great. Jilly is the greatest. And since the three of you have seen fit not to take advantage of that fact, I intend to. But I need some help."

"Help how?" Ned asked.

Kit looked at his three new friends affectionately. A month ago he would have written them off sight unseen as losers. Now he understood their values. They worked hard, much harder than their lazy manner suggested, but they didn't give a damn about wealth or social status. He could be himself with them. Whoever that was, these days.

"As you may have noticed," he proceeded doggedly, "Jilly is...shall we say skittish? No idea that she's gorgeous. No idea that I'm nuts about her. She sort of...shies away. I don't think it's me, though you guys should correct me if I'm wrong, at which point I'll kill you. I think it's Claude, that schmuck. I have to make some kind of a move sometime soon. And I need to know more about Claude, so I can figure out what move to make."

"Argh. Claude." Larry cowered in tipsy mock horror. "The Wimp Wonder."

"Mr. Comb-over," Jeff said in contempt.

"El Stuffed Shirt Supreme," Ned crowed.

"Uh, guys," Kit said, "what about a little hard information here? What did he do? What does he do, for that matter?"

"First things first," Jeff interrupted. "Malone, I hate to have to ask you this, but, you know, like, what are your intentions? Jilly is not some bimbo, and I, for one, am not helping you just, you know... You know."

"Yeah. I do know. And no. I mean, negative. I don't want to hurt Jilly. Why do you think I'm begging you idiots for information? Would I do that for a casual fling? I'm serious about her."

"Like how serious?" Larry asked suspiciously.

"Like very serious," Kit said, exasperated. "Very serious. Marriage serious. Maybe kids serious—although I'm not committing to that yet. Forever serious." Kit could feel his face get red and it ticked him off. He hadn't blushed since Mrs. Bogin had caught him with his hand up Elsie Smithers's skirt in sixth grade math.

Jeff thumped Kit on the back with half-drunken enthusiasm. "Okay, don't get agitated," he said. "We just don't want to be a party to some kind of disgusting one-night-stand hit-and-run seduction—"

"The kind of disgusting one-night-stand hit-and-run seduction, for example, that we do all the time," Ned interjected.

"Well, I'm not gonna do that," Kit said. "Hell, any fool

who thinks they could get enough of Jilly in just one night is...a fool."

"Well, congratulations, man," Ned said.

"We're happy. We're thrilled. Conch Team needs your spike. Marry Sanderson and we'll have it forever," Larry added with tipsy abandon. "Let's drink a toast to Killer and Jiller. I mean, Killy. Jilly. Whatever. Hey, Al! Yo! Another four Dos Equis, huh?"

The new bottles arrived and Kit took another sip of beer. He could feel the alcohol fogging his brain. Manfully he struggled to keep his focus. "So. Claude. What went on?"

"Well, we never actually met him," Larry began.

"You never actually met him?" Kit stared across the table at his so-called friends. "You conned me into making a total idiot of myself. You made me say the *M* word. And you never even met him? You're a bunch of goddamned goons."

"Jeez, Killer. Lighten up," Jeff complained.

"Really, Malone. We know this is important to you, but give us a chance, huh?" Larry was indignant.

"We didn't meet him, but we've seen him. And we've heard about him. We *know* him. Can't you understand that?" Ned whined.

"Yeah. All right, all right," Kit said. He could see they were trying to help. Besides, he'd suddenly gotten too tipsy to hold a grudge. He could feel his face sweating. Beer was probably running out of his pores. He closed his eyes, praying for concentration. "So?"

"So Claude put her down all the time," Jeff said, suddenly serious. "Her boobs were too small. Her brain was too big. She didn't dress right. She didn't talk right. Probably told her she didn't screw right, either. She never said that, but it figures."

"Yeah. You know the kind of thing," Ned said. "We all do it sometimes. But Claude did it all the time."

"Plus, Killer, the other thing is this. Jilly's family considers themselves to be a very big deal, socialwise. The Sandersons of Atlanta. Fancy. Formal. You know. Jilly never fit in, and they never let her forget it. So when Jilly marries Claude, she thinks she's finally gonna get a little love, a little approval, from her family, 'cause she married their idea of the perfect guy. Only it turns out she can't do a damn thing that pleases him, either. No matter how many times we all try to tell her, she still thinks there's something wrong with her. End of story." Larry stopped, out of breath.

"Yeah. End of story." Even through his beery haze Kit could see that the boys' analysis, however rough around the edges, made sense.

End of story, he thought. Except that Jilly's terrified. No wonder she thinks you're making fun of her when you tell her she's pretty. No wonder she doesn't want some slick urban type in a fancy suit to take over her life. No wonder her idea of male companionship is these three lovable and utterly unthreatening lunatics. No wonder she thinks men are selfish and arrogant and cruel.

Well, Malone, he thought fuzzily, bidding the guys goodnight and making his unsteady way up Simonton Street, *tonight you're just gonna have to change her mind.*

JILLY WALKED HOME from her dinner with Belle in a thoughtful mood. Simonton Street was quiet. The moon shone on the house roofs. Here and there lamps glowed through open-shuttered windows. Sometimes Jilly could see couples eating dinner, looking cozy and relaxed together.

She reached Truelove House quickly. To her dismay,

Kit's Jaguar was tucked under the mimosa in the driveway and the parlor blazed with light. He'd gone out with the guys and she'd hoped he would come home late. She was definitely ready to deal with her attraction to him, she thought nervously. Just not tonight.

"Kit?" she called, walking in through the hallway. There was no answer. She mounted the stairs in growing alarm. Maybe the inn had been visited by a real burglar.

It would be just her kind of luck if something horrible happened to Kit before she could even test her newfound nerve.

Instead, he was safe and fast asleep.

In jeans and sneakers and a faded Yale sweatshirt.

Propped up on the floor against her bedroom door, his long legs stretched out across the hallway's floral-patterned runner.

There was a tightly furled pink rose clutched in his right hand. Judging by the generous amount of stem, damp leaf and straggling root still attached to it, it had just been ripped from somebody's garden. She shuddered to think whose.

Silently she knelt beside him. "Kit?" she said softly, petting his arm. "Kit?"

"Jilly," he croaked, opening bleary eyes.

"Yes, Kit," she repeated, leaving her hand reassuringly on his arm.

"Jilly," he said urgently.

"What?" she asked gently, taking advantage of his half stupor to push a damp thick lock of hair from his forehead. *What a dope*, she thought. Normally she hated men who drank too much. But without really intending to she had come to trust him, at least a little. She knew that there must be a good reason for his inebriation tonight.

"You...need to...know," he mumbled, still looking into her brown eyes with his glassy pink-rimmed gray ones.

"What, silly? It's okay. Tell me."

"Jilly," he said earnestly, "I'm...very...serious."

With that he toppled over on his side, breathing heavily, and nothing she could do would rouse him.

Tugging the rose from his fingers, she stood up. She got a soft quilt from one of the guest rooms and tucked it around his hips. She kissed him on his damp forehead and went to bed, placing the rose carefully on the nightstand beside her.

He was drunk and disgusting and incoherent. She had no idea what this "serious" nonsense meant. She was still half convinced that he only cared for her like a sister.

But she didn't care.

She loved him.

Not lust, not mere attraction, not infatuation. Real love.

For better or for worse. For ecstasy or possible humiliation.

Helplessly, hopelessly, probably foolishly.

And the truth was that it just felt *good*.

6

JILLY WOKE AT EIGHT the next morning. The sun streamed through her window. She felt more alive than she'd felt in years. She no longer wanted something exciting to happen to her out of the blue, she realized. Now she was ready to do something exciting herself, like parachuting out of a plane or visiting Nepal or having great sex with Kit Malone.

Jilly tied the sash of her vintage robe around her waist and peered out of her room. Kit was no longer sleeping in the hallway. She padded quietly down the hall to the open door of his room. The shutters were closed. In the dim light, she could make out Kit's body lying on the floor.

He was sprawled on his back, breathing heavily, still wearing his jeans and sweatshirt. His hair was wildly tousled. His eyes were closed. She prodded his inert torso gently with her toe.

"Go away," he croaked.

"Are you okay?" she asked.

"No. Go away."

"Why are you lying on the floor?"

"Because I can't fall off it. Go away."

"I want to help."

"Go rescue a drowning puppy."

"No. I want to help *you*."

Raising his neck slightly, Kit winced. He laid his head back on the floor as carefully as if it were antique crystal.

Cracked antique crystal. "You can't. Trust me," he said. "Except by going away."

"Fine. Be that way. I'm going." Jilly went.

"I'm back," she said five minutes later, pushing open his door with her hip.

"So I hear. For a small girl, you have the tread of a bull elephant," he mumbled.

"Don't be nasty," Jilly said mildly. "Thousands of your brain cells may have died, but it's not my fault."

"Don't be so sure."

"What do you mean?" Jilly asked.

"Never mind. Now is not the time," Kit said.

Jilly opened the louvers of the shutters a fraction. She set the tray she was carrying on the floor and sat cross-legged next to it, making sure her bare legs were more or less discreetly covered.

Yup. Something had definitely changed, she thought. It wasn't just that she felt hale and hearty while the invincible Kit Malone was lying on the floor looking like beach debris. Now that she'd decided to throw caution to the winds, she no longer had to worry about what he was thinking or how to hide her own feelings. She had the upper hand, sort of. It was an invigorating idea.

"Breakfast," she announced.

"Spare me," Kit moaned. He sniffed as the fragrance of coffee hit his nostrils. On the tray sat two cups of black coffee, a plain baguette and a pink rose in a crystal bud vase.

"Hey," he said, peering at the rose through bloodshot eyes. "There are still roots on that thing."

"I went to your florist," Jilly said.

"Very funny. Don't yell." Grunting, Kit raised his aching torso from the floor and propped his back against the nightstand. He drew a trembling hand across his forehead and inspected it. Beer was still coming out of his pores.

"I'm speaking in a perfectly normal tone of voice. Here. Fresh-brewed French roast," Jilly said.

"Thanks." He wrapped his fingers around the steaming mug that Jilly handed him. "Actually, it tastes pretty good. But don't take it personally if I have to crawl to the bathroom and throw up."

"Of course not. No problem. Happens all the time. Tell me, though. Exactly how many beers did it take to accomplish this kind of hangover?"

"At least a hundred," Kit said. "Maybe more. Then tequila. Don't ask."

"Male bonding," Jilly said knowingly. "It's death."

"Jilly," Kit said, sighing, "I don't think I can stand to discuss gender issues right now."

"Okay by me. What do you want to talk about?"

"Nothing." Tentatively, Kit rolled his head a little, making sure that it was still attached to his neck. It was, but barely. "Let's just sit here and breathe."

Actually he decided a few minutes later, the coffee helped. So did Jilly's presence, however obnoxiously frisky she was being. He liked her there. He liked having her take care of him. He wouldn't even mind if she went a bit further. Kissed his aching forehead. Kissed the place where the hem of his sweatshirt met the waist of his jeans. Kissed a few other things, while she was at it. None of those parts actually ached, but what the hell.

Suddenly, as though the switch to his senses had just been flicked back on, he felt electrically aware of her half-naked body only a foot away. He looked her over under his lashes, deliberately keeping his eyes heavy lidded and half closed. He didn't see any evidence of a nightgown under the robe. The heavy fabric disclosed glimpses of her long brown legs and a triangle of creamy tanned skin where the lapels of the robe folded over. Underneath he

could just make out the gentle swell of her breasts and
hips.

Painfully he shifted his legs.

Thousands of his brain cells might be dead, he discovered, but other parts of him were definitely alive and kicking.

Which was just too bad for them, he decided. Having
waited this long, he was not about to ruin the tentative
trust they'd established with the kind of crude approach
that his body was urging right now. An amorous man was
one thing, an amorous, nauseous, hungover man was another. He might want to pull that robe of hers open and
push her onto the floor and have utterly mindless sex with
her, but he also wanted to court her. Win her heart. Possess
all of her, not just her body.

Besides, his breath probably smelled like swamp water.

He would get some more sleep and clean himself up.
Come home tonight and make her dinner and treat her like
a princess.

And then, of course, make love to her until they both
screamed with pleasure.

In the meantime, he might as well milk her comforting
presence for all it was worth.

"I don't feel good," he said pitifully, trying to look fragile.

"Too bad," Jilly answered.

"A minute ago you wanted to help me."

"I've had time to reconsider. Next time speak up
sooner," she said. There was no point in letting him get too
confident. Besides, she was not about to waste her seduction plans on a half-conscious man.

"I have a terrible, terrible headache. It would help if you
kissed my forehead, very gently, just once," he wheedled.

"No way," she said, standing up and taking the empty

cup from his hand. "You're an attractive guy, if you like
the type. But at the moment your skin is the color of mold,
and I'll bet your breath could take paint off a car."

"It was just a thought," Kit said in defeat, and closed his
eyes to sleep.

THE PHONE RANG AT three o'clock that afternoon, just as Kit
was trying to decide whether Jilly would like *boeuf bour-
guignon* or chicken *piccata* for dinner. "Truelove House,"
he answered.

"Malone?"

"Yeah."

"When the hell are you coming back?" said a squeaky
male voice.

"Oh. Hank. Don't talk so loud," Kit said, wincing. He
was feeling a lot better, but having Alvin the Chipmunk
yelling in his ear was the last thing he needed. "What's up?
How's the office? Did Angus MacPherson call?"

"Will you stop this Angus MacPherson obsession?"
Hank said at slightly lower volume. "Angus MacPherson
is only one of many potential clients. Which is just as well,
because he didn't call."

"Damn." Kit said. "There may be plenty of potential clients, but Angus is definitely the big fish. Do you realize he
could give us a hundred million bucks to manage and
barely notice it?"

"Malone, read my lips. You gave him your hire-us,
we're-the-best spiel three weeks ago. He hasn't called us.
He's probably not going to call us. The conclusion is obvious.   He-does-not-want-you-anywhere-near-his-money.
End of story. Let's move on, huh?"

"No way," Kit said. "The more elusive that crafty old
bastard acts, the more I want his business." He cradled the
receiver against his shoulder as he searched the kitchen

cupboard for bay leaves. He'd make the beef, he decided. It was too heavy for August, really, but he'd bought all the ingredients. He'd throw together a salad to lighten it up and distract her with a good wine. He leaned down and hauled a cast-iron pot onto the stovetop.

"Sure," Hank continued, oblivious to Kit's culinary preoccupations. "And what about the 112 clients who actually pay our salaries? No, make that 111, I forgot the Coles, who pulled their money out after you spat on their daughter. What are they, chopped liver?"

"I'm completely on top of their portfolios. I've been working from here, and you know it," Kit said mildly, rummaging through his sack of groceries for pearl onions. "In fact, I've made a number of very astute investments, and I pulled us out of that Megatech dog just in time. Not to mention Allied, which you may notice has rebounded nicely. Damn it. Sorry, not you, I just dropped an onion. Where'd that little sucker go? Oh, there it is. Under the sink, wouldn't you know?"

"Kit," Hank said, "I know you've been working the accounts. But that's not all you're supposed to do, and I'm tired of pretending it is. It's been over two weeks. The office is like a morgue, and the clients are beginning to look at me strangely when I make up lies about where my famous partner is. Even Mattie the plant lady is getting very morose. And all you can talk about is onions. Jeez. This is so humiliating. I sound like an abandoned wife trying to wheedle her roaming husband into returning to the homestead."

"You sure do," Kit teased, chopping. "Does Brenda know about your—uh—feelings for me? And how is Brenda, by the way?"

"Malone—"

"Sorry," Kit said apologetically. "I know it's not funny.

I know I'm being selfish. And I am coming back. In fact, let's pick a day. What's today?"

"August 20," Hank said.

"Okay. Look, Hank, nothing really happens Labor Day week, right? So I'll come back on that following Monday, September 8, how's that? Four weeks' vacation, that's not so bad, is it, for a partner of a firm?"

"This isn't your vacation, Malone. You took your vacation in December. And then there was that week in February when you just had to be in New York."

"That was work, I met with a client. At least once, if not more. Give me a break, Henry. You and Brenda have spent at least ten long weekends in the Caribbean in the past year. And this is next year's vacation I'm taking," Kit improvised.

Hank snorted. "Sure. September 8 is too late. I'll give you until the fourth. The Thursday after Labor Day. No longer."

Kit wiped his hands on the rear of his jeans. The fourth. Definitely a little soon, from the Jilly point of view. She wasn't going to be crazy about having a guy she'd just— hopefully—slept with hightailing it back to civilization so quickly. But the unusual grimness in Henry's voice told him he didn't have a choice. And he could always come back to Key West on weekends. Grimacing, he surrendered. "Fine. The fourth. I'll be there at 9:00 a.m. sharp. You better have something pretty damned important for me to do."

"Don't worry. I will." Kit could almost hear Hank relaxing over the phone. "So," Hank said, "don't be coy. Give me a progress report on the girl with the feminist cat."

"Well, let's see. She's tried to attack me with a shelf bracket. I've gone into a drunken stupor in front of her bedroom door. I think some of the stuff she's buying for the hotel rooms is going to get stolen and she thinks I'm wrong. She thinks plumbago will look good in the front garden and I know she's wrong. We've had fights in front of virtually everyone in Key West. But she looks damned cute in a bathrobe, and we have fun doing the crossword together."

"Wow," Hank breathed. "You didn't tell me you got married."

"Funny. Very funny," Kit said.

"You know the word that comes to mind?"

"What?" Kit said.

"Loser," Hank said. "Malone, you're a great swinging bachelor, and when you put your mind to it, you're an awesome stock picker. But as a serious contender for a committed relationship you are a total loser."

"I sure appreciate the vote of confidence. No wonder you're my best friend," Kit said, cubing the beef with savage strokes.

"Oh, it's not just my opinion," Hank continued blithely, seeming to savor his revenge. "Brenda thinks so, too, and my mother, and everyone on the secretarial staff. We all agree that you have as much chance of pulling off a real relationship with a normal everyday woman as Julia Roberts does of winning the world heavyweight boxing title."

Kit closed his eyes in frustration. Usually he enjoyed Hank's teasing, in a sick kind of way, but in this case it hit too close to home. What if Hank was right? Why did he think that his long history of meaningless flings had given him what it took to meet the demands of a serious relationship? "Is there anyone at all in greater Miami who believes in me?"

"Mattie. When she came in to mist and water the other day she told me that she'd marry you in a minute, pathological fear of intimacy and all."

"Well, that's something. If Jilly doesn't work out I can always console myself with a sixty-year-old widow in flowered carpet slippers. Can I hang up now, Hank?"

"Yup, we're done. Good luck. Seriously. I mean, you may be a loser, but you deserve the best." Kit could hear Henry laughing through the phone lines.

"I'm ever so grateful for your support," Kit said. "And Henry, don't forget."

"What?"

"Call me the minute you hear from Angus MacPherson. And trust me, loser or not, you will."

"THAT'S PRETTY," Belle said, looking at Jilly from her perch on a fitting-room bench.

"Too obvious," Jilly said. "Sequins strike the wrong note, I think. I want to seem available, but I don't want to seem easy."

"Oh, you're not easy," Belle said feelingly, slipping off her sandal and rubbing one aching foot.

Jilly paused in the middle of unzipping the dress and looked quizzically at her friend. "Had enough?" she asked.

"Are you kidding?" Belle smiled. "Better four exhausting hours among the dressing-room mirrors than an afternoon with my kids. But if I may say so, you are a tad picky."

"I'll know the right dress when I see it. I just haven't seen it yet."

"We've been to every single store in Key West. Jilly, you're having a guy to dinner, not accepting an Academy Award."

"I want to feel confident," Jilly said, pulling the next dress off its hanger.

"Try therapy, or maybe a lobotomy," Belle advised. "Trust me. For your problem, one dress is not enough."

"Ho-ho. What do you think of this?"

"It sets off your waist, which I envy, since mine is probably about to go down for the third and final time. But that shade of aqua makes you look sort of like the Queen Mum on a bad day."

"I *hate* shopping. Have I told you that?" Jilly yanked the dress down over her hips.

"Often. And loudly."

"Sorry. Oh, well. Let's go next door, and if there's nothing there we'll move on to the Ocean Grille, where I'll have a glass of champagne and you'll have a lemonade, just in case you're pregnant."

"Don't remind me," Belle said faintly, following Jilly out of the store. "I really can't cope with your dress and the thought of giving birth to more twins at the same time."

AT FIVE-THIRTY, KIT STOOD in the middle of the kitchen and reviewed his progress.

Very fancy beef stew, finished and simmering in its pot. Check. And if he did say so himself, it smelled damned good.

Wine, a nice robust red, waiting to be uncorked. Check.

Table set. Check. Not elegant, but welcoming, with candles to soften the mood. And he'd even run out to get flowers—real, honest cut-by-a-florist flowers—for a centerpiece.

Soft music. Check. Classical guitar on tape, on a boom box plugged in behind the kitchen counter.

Parlor, neatened up and lit with a few small lamps. Bedroom—his—cleaned up, which he hoped Jilly would appreciate. Condoms in the bedroom drawer. Clean towels in the bathroom. Check.

Half humming in anticipation, he lowered the flame under the stew pot and let the kitchen door shut softly behind him. He settled himself on the parlor floor to sort through a crate of antique lighting fixtures he'd bought at an auction that afternoon, marveling at the astonishing turn his life had taken. Who would have thought that he'd be so happy just sitting around, making dinner and waiting for a beautiful but eccentric woman in baggy clothes to walk through the door? Maybe Hank and the rest of the population of greater Miami were wrong. Maybe this was really going to work. He got out a can of brass polish and began rubbing at one of the old lamps, looking at his watch as he sat down again on the parlor floor. Six. She'd probably be home any minute. The mere thought made him happy.

By six-thirty, he was getting concerned about the dinner. Nervously he lowered the flame under the stew another notch and covered the bowl of salad more tightly.

By seven, he was concerned about Jilly. This absence was unlike her. Unless she had something planned—in which case she almost always mentioned it to him—she was always home by now. Reaching for the phone he dialed the shop, but no one was there. It was probably irrational, he knew, but he couldn't help but worry.

By eight, concern had been replaced by irritation. He'd been sitting around for hours, he thought in self-pity. And he'd worked so hard on dinner. He turned off the flame under the stew, and knowing the gesture to be childish, yanked the flowers from their vase and threw them away.

By nine, he was furious. He knew it was unfair to be so mad. He couldn't exactly remember confirming their plans for dinner, so maybe it was an innocent misunderstanding. But it didn't matter. Like a runaway mustang, his temper had bolted too fast and too far to call back. He could almost feel the days of hope and anxiety and forbearance and sexual frustration thundering inside his head, and what was worse, he didn't even want to stop the stampede.

His jaw clenched, he dumped the contents of the stew pot into storage containers, unset the table and put the wine back in the wine closet where it belonged. Changing his mind, he took it out and poured himself a glass. Changing his mind again, he dumped the glassful of liquid into the sink. Whatever happened, he decided grimly, he wasn't going to get drunk. If Jilly thought she could just walk all over his stuporous body tonight, she was in for a surprise. Slamming the kitchen door behind him, he strode to the parlor and sat down on its highest, straightest, stiffest chair. Crossing his arms, ignoring the open can of brass polish and the TV and the books and magazines that dotted the room, he settled in to wait.

Fifteen minutes later, Jilly bounced in.

She was wearing a coppery brown silk tank top that showed off her beautiful shoulders and a slim black skirt that hugged her hips and stopped well short of her tanned knees. She had on little strappy black sandals and big black hoop earrings. Her tawny hair tumbled around her face. Her cheeks were flushed, her lips rosy. She looked happy. Alive. Glowing. As though she'd just been kissed. As though she was in love.

No way. No way in hell. It's the wind, Kit thought in panic. *Sure, fool,* he answered himself immediately. *The wind. You're pathetic.*

"Hey, Malone," Jilly said happily, throwing her shopping bags on a chair. "Your face isn't green anymore. Does that mean you're feeling better?"

Brotherly, Kit cursed silently. *Brotherly. Some joke. The woman of my dreams comes in looking like she's just had a hot date with the man of* her *dreams, and she treats me like a chum.*

So much for those days of restraint. Who was it who said that no good deed ever goes unpunished? "Peachy," he said grimly. "Have a good night?"

"Great," Jilly said. "Wonderful. What's all this?"

Kit looked at the evening's project without enthusiasm. "Some light fixtures. I thought we could use them for the hallways."

"Wow. Kit, these are great. I bet they're just like the sconces the house originally had." Jilly kicked off her shoes and knelt on the floor, poking through the tangle of hardware. Deliberately she kept her back to Kit, trying to hide the delight on her face. It was so sweet of him to buy the fixtures, and it was the first time he'd ever done something on the inside—her part—of the inn. Plus, he had good taste. Things were definitely looking up here. "Where did you find these things? Did you spend all evening polishing them?"

"I bought them at the auction house in Tavernier," he said, keeping his voice neutral with a massive effort of will. "There's some stew in the oven."

"Thanks," Jilly said cheerfully. "I ate already, but we can save it for lunch."

"Where did you go?" Kit leaned against the mantelpiece as he spoke, trying to rest his clenched fists casually on its surface, as though it were an ordinary night and an ordinary question.

Sure, he thought. *Just your ordinary everyday interrogation.*

"Chalfont's." Jilly was still absorbed in the sconces.

Chalfont's, Kit thought. Perfect. Chalfont's. Spectacular ocean view, sexy atmosphere, stratospheric prices. It was not the kind of place a woman out on a date with the wind would choose.

"The white chocolate mousse was great," she added innocently.

I bet his kisses were better. Damn him, Kit thought.

He'd always known that to win her he'd have to battle the pain of her past and the betrayal of her ex-husband and his own idiotic behavior. But another lover, no. Never, ever had it occurred to him that he might have to compete against an actual flesh-and-blood man.

"Well," he said, his resentment finally erupting, "I'm very glad you managed to feed yourself so well. The pitiful little excuse for dinner I worked on all afternoon certainly pales in comparison."

"I didn't know you were making dinner," she said. She looked up at his face, baffled, with an innocence that somehow made him even angrier.

"I didn't know you were eating out," he said. "Stop fiddling with that thing."

Jilly handed him the sconce she was holding and straightened up. "I didn't know I had to tell you. Anyway, the last time I saw you I *couldn't* tell you, since you were practically unconscious."

Kit dropped the sconce back into the box and brushed off his hands, clapping them together with loud angry gestures. "You don't. You don't have to tell me anything. Who am I to expect to know your plans? Anyway, from now on I'll just assume you'll be out with Gary."

"Who?"

"Paul. Ralph. Tom. Dick," Kit said. "Harry. Whoever it was who fed you white chocolate mousse and put those sexy little roses in your cheeks."

"Not that it's any of your business, but I went shopping with Belle and I ate dinner by myself and I walked all the way home. I was in a good mood. Was, you notice. God, Kit. What is *wrong* with you? So my cheeks are red. It's windy."

"Sure. It's a veritable sirocco out there," he snapped.

"Not that I would know. I've been inside, cooking and waiting for you."

Jilly's patience finally gave out. "Don't play the martyr with me, you big spoiled brat," she said, her eyes narrowing. "I didn't ask you to make dinner. I didn't ask you to sit around and wait. And just for the record, you don't own me."

"No, I don't," Kit spat. "That privilege belongs to Tom or Dick. But maybe he'll let me borrow you once in a while, just so we can get this renovation done."

Jilly opened her mouth to speak. Instead, she clenched her jaw, stuck her hands on her hips and looked at him.

He stood facing her, shoulders tensed, and waited for her to say something. But she just looked at him some more.

When she finally spoke, her voice was dangerously quiet. "You know, Malone, a couple of weeks ago I would have assumed the worst about this. But I've gotten to know you a little, and I've learned that you're actually a pretty nice guy. So I'm going to trust that there is some reason that you're acting this way. A mistaken reason, obviously. Probably an idiotic reason. But a reason. So instead of screaming at you, I'm just going to tell you one thing before I call it a night."

She picked up her shopping bags and jacket and stood a foot or so away from him, looking fearlessly up into his eyes. "That one thing is this. Whatever your reason, whatever you're thinking, you are making a complete and utter fool of yourself. You owe me an apology."

Jilly, I love you. Love me. "That's two things, actually," he said.

"Complete. And utter," Jilly said to him. She turned on her heel and headed for the door. He could hear her soft footfalls as she climbed the stairs.

Well, at least she's not bouncing anymore, he thought.

That should have made him happy, but it didn't.

Cursing, he strode over to the parlor's largest window and wrenched it open. He stomped over to the pile of brass sconces and furiously but methodically began to throw them out into the garden, as hard as he could.

When the last fixture was gone, he slammed the window shut. The bottom of the pane of hundred-year-old beveled glass cracked. He rested his forehead on the cool unbroken stretch at the top.

She was right. When it came to this serious emotional stuff, she almost always was.

He was making a fool of himself.

If she didn't have a lover, his accusations were cheap and demeaning. If she did, they were cheap, demeaning and pointless. Acting like a jealous maniac was not going win her back.

What had happened to his wish to court her, to win her trust?

And the truth was that hard as he tried, he couldn't say for sure that he had actually asked her to dinner.

Hank is right, he thought. *I'm a loser.* But self-pity wasn't going to help.

He went into the kitchen and assembled a tray, pulling a few uncrushed blooms out of the garbage for a bud vase. Upstairs, he knocked gently on her door.

"It's me. Can I come in?"

There was a silence, then a soft assent. Jilly was sitting in bed, wearing one of her big white T-shirts and a wary expression.

"Um," Kit said. "I thought you might like some tea."

"Thank you," she said quietly. "Want to sit down?"

Kit sat hesitantly at the edge of the bed.

"Want some?" she asked, holding up the pot. He shook

his head. "Did you finish, uh, how shall I put it—planting the lamps in the garden?" she asked.

"Yeah." He looked at her calm face, finding no words to say.

"Just think. If you leave them there a few days, maybe they'll grow into chandeliers," she said, smiling at him.

"Jilly," he said helplessly. "Jilly, I'm sorry for acting like a jerk. But I did have a reason. A stupid reason, I admit. But a reason."

Jilly took his hand in hers, entwining her slim fingers in his strong ones. "I know. It's okay."

"Don't you want to know what it was?"

"Eventually. Not right now. It doesn't matter at the moment." She smiled at his doubtful expression. "You're forgiven. Absolved. A blanket pardon."

Moodily Kit looked down at their linked hands. Hers looked so little, so delicate clasped in his. "It's too easy. It doesn't work that way between men and women. Now is the time you're supposed to make me crawl. If you're actually nice about it, you're just going to make me feel guiltier."

"Don't. I'm not doing this for you. At least, not only for you. I just think we've both had long days, and it's late, and we don't need more...fireworks...right now." Jilly smiled and squeezed his hand. "If you don't want a pardon, we'll make it a temporary reprieve. I promise to yell at you tomorrow, if your explanation doesn't cut the mustard. Deal?"

"Deal," Kit said, lifting her hand and depositing a quick warm reasonably brotherly kiss on the back of it.

"Listen," Jilly said. "Saturday is my thirty-third birthday. I hate birthdays, so I never tell anyone about mine. But I was wondering if you'd like to come to my house. I'll cook dinner. You know, to celebrate. If you don't have plans."

"Your birthday? Saturday?" Kit said, surprised. "I could have sworn you were a spring baby."

"Nope. August 23," Jilly said, surreptitiously crossing the fingers of the hand Kit wasn't holding. "Anyway. No big deal. You're probably busy."

"No. Of course I'm not busy," Kit said. "But are you sure you want to stay home and cook? Why don't you let me take you out?"

"No. No, it's—it's a kind of tradition with me. Since I hate birthdays and don't cook much the rest of the year. You know," Jilly stuttered. *Jilly, shut up. Now.*

"Well, okay," Kit said. "What can I do to help? At least let me bring something."

"I don't know," Jilly said. "Yes, I do. You can bring roses for the table. Make sure they still have the thorns and roots on—I've gotten to like them that way. But don't steal them from the guy two doors down—he gave me a very peculiar look the other day."

Kit smiled at her. For a moment they were both silent. Shyly silent, hesitantly silent, like teenagers.

"Well, then," Kit said, awkwardly.

"Well," Jilly answered, suddenly self-conscious. "I guess we should get some sleep. Don't worry anymore, all right? We can fight about it tomorrow."

Kit released her hand and stood up. She had forgiven him, and she was probably right about not getting into it tonight, but this felt so...flat. Unfinished. "Yeah," he said, looking down at her, trying to sound cheerful. "I'd better be up early enough to grab those sconces before someone else does."

"Yes," Jilly said. Her heart swelled with tenderness for him. "Um...Kit?"

"What?"

"I have a terrible, terrible headache. It would help if you would kiss my forehead, very gently, just once."

Kit's heart leapt with relief. He sat carefully down on the bed again. Cradling her face in his hands, he leaned over and dusted her forehead with his lips. He kissed the tip of her nose, then her cheek. Then he kissed her mouth, letting his lips rest on hers for a moment, breathing in the scent of her hair and the smoothness of her skin until he was dizzy. He could feel her relax hesitantly against him and the hint of surrender made his heart pound. Clasping his hands around her shoulders he leaned more closely against her and she leaned back, bringing her arms up around his back, hesitantly opening her lips under his. He could feel her soft firm breasts under the thin cotton of her nightshirt, feel the pounding of her heart. Her mouth was warm and soft and tasted faintly of white chocolate mousse. Gently he angled his mouth and licked his tongue against hers, loving the intimacy of kissing her, loving the way she kissed him back.

It was delicious, kissing Jilly. He wanted to do it forever. Slowly, carefully, he pulled himself away.

God, he wanted to make love to her.

God, he didn't want to blow this.

Saturday, his eyes told her.

Saturday, her eyes answered. *I think*.

"Thank you, Kit," she said huskily. "Good night."

"Good night, Jilly," he said, and with a superhuman effort left the room.

7

JILLY SPENT THE HOURS until Saturday evening in a daze, distracted and edgy. She attempted to act like a normal person, more or less. She ran her shop, finished ordering the new curtains and area rugs for Truelove House, kept Maisie DuMaurier from changing her mind about her dining room chairs, played a good game of volleyball and even managed to pick a few fights with Kit, just to keep things ordinary.

Inside, she was a mess. She wished she hadn't told Kit Saturday, it seemed so far away. It seemed so close. In fact, she wished she hadn't asked Kit to dinner in the first place. What if he wasn't attracted to her, after all? What if he showed up in jeans and a sweatshirt and offered to order pizza? What if he thought her dress looked dumb? What if they didn't make love? What if they made love and it was lousy? What if they made love and it was great?

What is your problem, Jillian Mabel Sanderson? she asked herself, wandering through Truelove House's half-renovated bedrooms. *It's not the key battle of a world war. It's not the final laboratory test of the cure for cancer. It's a date, Jilly. A date. People do it all the time and survive. Some people even think dates are fun. They're sick puppies, but still... Why are you being such a baby?*

"Oh, shut up," she said aloud. Resolutely she walked downstairs, determined to get her mind off Kit.

"I love you, Jilly, go away," Margaret said, deep in a stack of bills on Thursday morning.

"Hey, babe," Ned said, helping Kit and Larry and Jeff move a vanload of antique armoires into Truelove House on Thursday afternoon. "Could you stand over there? You're kind of blocking the way. In fact, why don't you go paint a wall or something? This is men's work."

"Oh, shut up," Jilly muttered to his back.

"I've definitely decided on the white tile with the green borders for the kitchen," Maisie DuMaurier said, sitting in Jilly's shop on Friday morning.

"That's great, Maisie," Jilly said with a sigh of heartfelt thanks. At this rate, Maisie's house might even be finished by the turn of the century or so. A thought struck her. "Why don't you let me buy you a glass of champagne to celebrate?" she asked.

"I'd love to, Jilly! But couldn't we make it later? I've got a million things to do," Maisie said.

"No one wants to be with me," Jilly complained, passing Kit in the hallway of Truelove House early on Friday evening.

"I do," Kit said. *With you. On top of you, even. I'm easy,* he added silently.

"You don't count," Jilly said.

"Fine. Then I don't want to be with you, either," he answered agreeably.

"Fine. I do have things to do." Jilly stuck out her chin, irrationally offended.

"Women," Kit mused, climbing the stairs in his usual two-at-a-time fashion. "Can't please 'em, can't understand 'em, can't live with 'em, can't shoot 'em."

"Oh, shut up," Jilly muttered under her breath, heading out the door.

"I heard that," Kit said from the stairs.

FINALLY, SATURDAY evening came. To her surprise, Jilly found that her anxiety had been replaced with a kind of fatalistic numbness. She didn't feel bad anymore, just sort of blank, with a premonition of doom. *Napoleon just before Waterloo*, she thought. *Johnstown just before the flood.*

Sighing, she slipped into her high-heeled pumps and surveyed herself in the mirror on her bedroom door. She did look good, she admitted to herself. It was a fabulous dress, and she'd actually blown her hair dry rather than just scrunching it up with her fingers. She was even wearing heels, which in her opinion was kind of like volunteering for a spell on a medieval rack. Kit might turn out to have no real interest in her, but no one could say she hadn't done her best.

She switched out all of the upstairs lights except the small stained glass lamp in the bedroom and walked carefully down the stairs. From the bottom step she surveyed her home. After three weeks at Truelove House her place seemed very tiny, very feminine and very, very personal. There were bookshelves filled to bursting with all of her favorite art books, small oil paintings she had collected over the years, patchwork pillows she'd sewn from scraps of old fabric. She'd done it all herself, all with loving care. *This house is my haven, my safe place, my nest, my refuge*, she thought in panic. *Kit Malone will not fit in here. Inviting him home is about as smart as asking Bonnie and Clyde to cash my paycheck for me.*

And then the doorbell rang. When she opened the door, Kit stepped into her living room, looking perfectly at home there amid her chintzes and bric-a-brac, as though he'd lived with her for a million years.

"Hello, Jilly," he said in that deep resonant voice of his.

"Hello, Kit," she said, looking at him.

He had just shaved and his hair was still damp at the

temples, she noticed, attuned to everything about him. He was wearing black pleated pants and a black linen jacket, and underneath it, an ivory crew-neck pullover in some kind of thick silky fabric. As usual he looked devastatingly handsome, utterly male and dangerously sexual. One hand was hooked with lazy elegance in his jacket pocket. The other held a small, tight bouquet of pale pink tea roses, which he handed to her as she watched.

"Roses," she said inanely, taking them. "And in tissue, too."

"I had to buy them at a florist's," Kit told her. "None of the neighbors had anything nice."

"They're beautiful." Suddenly Jilly felt the sensuality of the moment wash over her like a tidal wave. The moist sweet fragrance of the flowers, mingled with the tang of Kit's aftershave. The soft lights downstairs. The thought of the bedroom upstairs, of Kit's lean hard body driving against hers on her big soft bed. She felt her face flush. She buried her nose in the bouquet, feeling shy, hoping her blush didn't show.

Kit watched Jilly's soft cheek rest against the velvety roses and tried not to lose his mind.

Who was it, a voice in his brain sneered, *who decided this woman was not your type?*

Who was it who kept dismissing her as kind of cute?

Who was it who decided to waste three weeks acting brotherly?

Whoever it was, he thought, trying not to grab her, *he's a total, unmitigated, irredeemable ass.*

The woman before him was no tomboy. She was a goddess, small and slender, poised and regal, graceful and proud.

The woman before him was not cute, or pretty, or appealing, or even quirkily attractive. She was beautiful, pe-

riod. Gorgeous, in fact. Hers was a heartstoppingly lovely
face, Kit realized, and he couldn't believe that he had managed to lust after her for so long without fully acknowledg-
ing that fact.

Jilly was wearing a black dress with long sleeves, a high
neck and a slim straight skirt that ended just above her
perfect knees. It had small black satin bows at its narrow
wrists, bows which matched the tiny bows on her black
pumps. It was a tasteful well-mannered dress, Kit thought,
the kind of dress she could have worn to any society party
without causing so much as a single remark. But somehow
the combination of the dress and her slim, gently curved
figure and her long legs in their sheer black hose was anything but sedate.

"Happy birthday, Jilly," he said. He put his hands in his
jacket pockets and clenched his fists.

Momentarily startled, she looked at him, then remembered. "Oh. Thanks." She blinked. "I should put these in
water. Why don't you sit down? Would you like a glass of
wine?" Kit nodded. Jilly turned away from him toward the
kitchen, and Kit's jaw dropped.

From the back, her little black dress wasn't sedate at all.
There was a neat black satin bow at the nape of her neck
and a matching one at the back of the fitted waist. In between the two there was nothing but smooth, silky, tanned
skin, enticingly punctuated with the gentle swell of her
spine and the angles of her delicate shoulder blades.

It's a back, buddy, Kit told himself desperately. *You've seen
them before.*

No. It's not a back. It's the *back.*

Okay. Okay. You can have her, he promised himself. Just
not before dessert.

He paced around the living room while he waited for
her to return with the wine. The house was pretty and per-

sonal. It would have made him feel cozy and at home, if he hadn't been crazed for sex.

"I brought you a gift," he blurted when Jilly returned. "For your birthday." He handed her a box from his pocket and took a sip from his wineglass, letting the fruity liquid wet his parched mouth.

Awkwardly Jilly set her own wineglass on the sofa table and opened the small velvet box. Inside, two earrings, small round opals ringed with tiny bands of diamonds, rested on a blue velvet bed. Jilly felt her eyes moisten. She looked up at Kit, wordless.

"They were Lavinia's," Kit said. "Do you like them?"

"I love them."

"Come here, then, sweetheart," Kit said softly. "I'll put them on for you."

Hesitantly she stepped closer to him and held out the box. His warm fingers caressing her, he slid off her small pearl studs and slipped one of the opals into a pierced lobe. "I've never done this for a woman before," he said, his voice husky.

"How do you know so well what to do?"

"I used to wear an earring myself." Kit slipped the second earring back into place and held her face in his hand. "They look beautiful on you."

She turned her cheek against his palm and smiled at him. "You wore an earring?" she teased, her voice barely above a whisper. His face was so close to hers that she could see the tiny creases on the outside of his eyes and feel his warm breath.

"A little silver hoop. Back in the days when I was a beachcomber. I always wanted a gold one, but by the time I could afford it I'd grown out of the idea. See? Right here." Kit took her hand and guided it to his left lobe. Sure enough, there was a slight dimple where his ear had been pierced. Jilly touched it wonderingly with the pad of her index finger.

"I think a small gold earring on an attractive man is very sexy," she said, her voice still low.

"Mmm? What else do you think is sexy?"

Jilly paused. "Long legs in worn jeans. Broad shoulders. Wavy dark hair." She took a deep breath. "Strong opinions." She breathed in again. "You. I find you sexy," she said, "Malone."

Kit's gray eyes looked steadily into her brown ones. Without judgment or deceit. With approval and passion and—Jilly thought in wonder—with what looked like love.

"Sanderson," he whispered, "I find you sexy, too. Very sexy."

"Really?" Some wounded old part of her still hesitated. "You've been so...casual with me. Sexless. Chummy."

Kit's finger traced the angle of her jaw, the delicate whorl of her ear, the curve of her lips. "Believe me, beautiful," he said, his voice wry, "it wasn't easy."

"Then...why?"

"Because what you yelled at me that first night was true. I was arrogant. I was careless. I was selfish." He took a deep breath. "Because I wanted to take the time to show you—hell, I don't know—that I was more than just a guy looking for sex. That I would be sticking around, if you wanted." He stopped and Jilly watched a wave of deep, brooding unhappiness sweep across his strong features. He dropped his eyes and shrugged his shoulders helplessly. "I want you more than I've ever wanted a woman. But I don't want to hurt you, Jilly," he said.

Jilly was astonished by the depth of feeling on his face. The Kit she knew rarely showed pain. One day soon, she wanted to find out where it came from. But not now, she thought. Not now.

"I'm a big girl, Kit. You're not going to hurt me, and I'm glad you gave me time," she said softly. "But let's not wait anymore."

"That's fine with me." He cupped her shoulders in his large strong hands, letting the tips of his fingers touch the warm bare skin of her back. "Are there any simmering pots or pans we need to turn off?"

"No," she said, her voice breathless and shaky. "I had a catering company deliver the whole thing, right down to the wine. It's all still sitting in the kitchen in little foil cartons."

"I'm glad," Kit said, an undertone of laughter in his voice. "Then...we can heat it up anytime."

"Anytime," she promised. "Anytime at all."

Wordlessly Kit lifted her into his arms. "Then there's two things you need to teach me," he said. "The first is, where's your bedroom?"

Jilly rested her head against his shoulder, savoring the feeling of being held. "Upstairs," she said. "First door on the left." Effortlessly Kit carried her up the tiny old stairs, setting her gently upright on the rug in her room. The light from the small stained glass lamp enveloped them in a warm rosy glow.

"What's the second thing?" she whispered, nestling against him, slipping her arms under his jacket and clasping them behind his back.

"The second thing is, how do I get this gorgeous dress off you?"

"It's simple, silly. You just untie the bows." Deliberately, slowly, she pivoted, holding her arms out from her sides, offering him the ribbons at her nape and waist and wrists. As he watched she trembled, a quick shiver of anxiousness and passion, but she stood trustingly still, silently telling him that she was ready, as ready as he was at last.

Kit sat on the edge of the bed and put his hands on her hips. Slowly, he bent his head and began to kiss her back, touching her with light butterfly kisses that barely grazed her skin and then tasting her more roughly, licking at her, first the nape of her neck and then the top of her spine and then her shoulder blades. The places he kissed were wet and then warm and then cold when his warm mouth left them, making her shiver. She could never have imagined the pleasure his kisses gave her, never have believed that something as simple as a man's mouth on her shoulders could make her so hungry, never have conceived that her world could become this small, just Kit's body and her body and their explosive need. Suddenly all she could think about was the places he was touching her—and the places he wasn't, her hips and her breasts and her thighs and the hot tense place between her legs.

Jilly grasped his hands and gave a soft, imploring whimper. Twisting to face him, she perched sideways on his lap. Kit put his arms around her and turned her head and brought his face to hers, kissing her deeply for what some part of her mind registered wonderingly was the first time. His mouth was hot and tasted slightly, enticingly of wine. Cautiously at first, then urgently, she kissed him back, lacing her fingers through his thick black hair, rubbing her face against the roughness of his jaw, opening her lips so that he could lick and nip and stroke her with his tongue, licking and nipping and stroking him back.

Jilly felt hot and liquid and mindless, as though she was nothing but the sweet ache of her body, the feeling of Kit against her was the only reality that existed. She arched against him and he brought one hand from her back to her breast, cupping its softness through the fabric of her dress,

rubbing her nipple with his thumb. Deftly he slipped his
other hand beneath her short skirt. Gasping, Jilly slid her
thighs open, wanting his hand against her, feeling him
moan when he discovered the lacy tops of her black stockings and the hot bare flesh above.

"Jilly," he groaned, standing, pulling her upright
against him, his face tense with need. Urgently he pulled
the satin ribbons at her right wrist, then her left, then the
wider bow that caught the dress at her waist and the short
zipper below it, and finally the black ribbon at her nape.
The soft fabric dropped from her shoulders and he let it
fall, eased it off her hips, helped her step away as it pud-
dled on the floor. She stood facing him, wearing only the
earrings he had given her, her black stockings and panties,
her delicate satin pumps. "God, Jilly," he breathed, taking
in her high small breasts, endless legs and flat, creamy
belly. "You are so damned beautiful. So perfect."

"Kit," she breathed, reaching for him. "Now. I need
you, now."

"Yes, beauty, now." Quickly he lifted her onto the bed.
He stood beside her and pulled off his clothes, shrugging
fluidly out of his jacket, dropping his sweater on the floor,
reaching into the pocket of his slacks for protection before
kicking out of them, never taking his mesmerizing gray
eyes off hers, his gaze intense and steady and so intimate
she felt it in her bones. He was drinking her in and she did
the same to him, staring into his eyes, looking boldly at his
body, reveling in her need for him, in their need for each
other. Even hurrying, he was graceful, every movement
strong and confident. His naked body was magnificent,
much more beautiful than the most fevered of her imagin-
ings, big and tough and long muscled and urgently
aroused. Just looking at him made her wild, made her
tense with desire.

She made a low helpless sound in her throat, arched her back and lifted her hands to him. He sat at the side of the bed for a moment, his back to her. "One minute, sweetheart," he breathed. "All right, now," and suddenly he was in her arms, powerful and heated, and they were rolling against each other on her bed, his hips pushing against her, his hands lifting her long stockinged legs until they were wrapped tightly around his waist. He slid one hand between them and reached between her thighs to where she was slick and wet for him, stroking her swollen flesh until she gasped against his mouth. When he slipped inside her she cried out in shock at the hardness of him, the fullness. And then he was pinioning her beneath him, rocking into her, steady and hot and rhythmic, rocking back and forth, again and again, and she was loving him back, as wild and fearless and out of control as he was. She could feel her body spasm with pleasure and completion, his body exploding inside her, and they were rocking against each other still, slower, quieter, softer, never wanting to let go.

KIT LAY ON HIS BACK, his tanned skin damp, cradling Jilly protectively in his arms. Jilly was curled on her side, her head on his chest, one leg tangled with his, the other stretched across his waist. Kit stroked her hip and back, exhausted and disbelieving. "It's never like that," he said, closing his eyes in surrender. He angled his neck to kiss the top of her head. "I didn't think it was even possible. Don't tell anybody."

"I know. I won't," Jilly murmured sleepily. "It's our secret."

Their lovemaking had been everything she'd ever imagined. No, more. In her heart of hearts she had always believed that all the books and the movies and the magazine articles lied, that physical passion could never be the fireworks and frenzy they described. At least not for her. But Kit had proved her wrong. The lovemaking between them had been rapturous and yet playful. Primal—at times even rough—and yet tender. An explosive merging between two purely physical creatures and an intimate, knowing, wholly personal embrace.

"Kit?" she whispered against his neck.

"Yes, sweetheart?"

"I have a confession to make." Gently she kissed the damp, springy hair at the center of his chest. "I am a spring baby, just like you thought. March 30th, in fact."

"Mmm?" Puzzled, he ran his hand lazily over the curve of her bottom.

"It's not my birthday today, Kit. I just wanted an occasion to dress sexy for you. Privately." She gave a drowsy giggle. "You can take the earrings away now if you want."

"You witch." He grinned, then laughed aloud, so pleased with her and himself and the world he thought he would burst. "You gorgeous little hussy. There's a wicked woman under all that tomboy stubbornness, isn't there?"

"Mmm. Sure seems to be." Jilly turned on her side, pulling him to face her, pressing herself against his warmth. She felt safe, and contented, and once again aroused. Life with Kit Malone was going to be a torment, she thought, if hours of lovemaking just left her wanting more. "And now that the wanton woman in me has been unleashed," she teased, tilting her head back to look into his eyes, "who knows when she might appear again?"

"Any time she wants, sweetheart," Kit said. "In fact, how about now?"

"No." Jilly curled her legs around his thighs and smiled.

"No?"

"No. It's too soon. I read it somewhere. I'm in my sexual

prime, but you're way past yours. Men your age need longer in between. I want to, but it's a physical impossibility."

"Really?" Kit pulled her hips against him so that she could feel his hardness, proving her wrong.

"Oh. No. I mean yes. Yes, there," she breathed, no longer teasing. "Like that. Oh, Kit. You're right. This is crazy. It can't be like this."

"It's okay," he whispered, holding her close. "It's our secret. I'll never tell."

IT WAS MORNING. The quick hard rain of the Keys beat on the roof of Jilly's little house and the wind whipped the branches of the trees. Jilly, awakening first, sat carefully up in bed. She looked down at her body in wonder. There was a tiny blue bruise where her breast met her arm. Tracing it with her finger she shivered happily, remembering. She had never been the kind of girl that men nibbled at in ecstasy. Luckily, though, Kit Malone hadn't figured that out.

She pulled up the sheet, wrapped her arms around her raised knees and looked down at Kit. He was sprawled on his back, his body slanted across her bed, his legs stretched out. His arm was flung over his face, hiding his eyes. Below it she could see his dark-stubbled chin and his mouth, beautifully shaped even in the relaxation of sleep. His chest rose and fell rhythmically. Taking advantage of his oblivion, Jilly feasted her eyes on the smooth tanned breadth of his shoulders, the intimate curve of pale flesh under his arm, the tightly muscled, impossibly narrow waist. The sheet covered him up to his navel. Stealthily, she tugged it downward an inch, stopping to check his face and make sure he was still asleep.

He lay there, breathing slowly. Motionless. Grinning.

Blushing, Jilly yanked the sheet up and smacked him on the hip.

"Hey," he said, rolling over and capturing her underneath him. "I was kind of enjoying that."

"You're conceited enough already. I don't want to make it worse," Jilly whispered, nuzzling the place where his black curls tumbled onto his neck. Luxuriously she ran her hands down his sides, feeling the silky surfaced muscles of his ribs, cupping her hands around the tautness of his waist. "Though I do have to tell you, Malone, you have a terrific body."

"So do you, Sanderson," he said. "Absolutely world-class."

"Not like yours."

"No, thank goodness.' Kit laughed. "Jilly, are you happy?"

"Yes," she said honestly, kissing his throat. "Completely, insanely happy."

"Me, too," he said huskily. "You make me happy. In fact, I cannot believe how happy you make me." Slowly, erotically, he ran his fingertips down her sides.

Shivering with pleasure, Jilly craned her neck to look at the bedside clock. "Kit," she said reluctantly.

"Mmm?" Kit bent his head to kiss her breast. She was unbelievable, he thought dreamily. They were unbelievable, together. His words to her the previous night had been no lie. It had never been like this for him, never so hot or so tender, never so complete.

"Kit," she said again, helplessly, twisting away from his touch. He looked up, concerned. "I want this, too," she said, breathing hard. "I mean, I don't ever want to get up. I feel dumb interrupting. But I'm expecting the inn's new pillows to be delivered, and UPS always gets to Truelove House right at nine."

Kit's eyes traveled from her beautiful breasts, which were flushed and aroused, to her beautiful face, which was tense and worried. He cuddled her to his chest and kissed her mouth gently. "It's all right, sweetheart. We can wait. Okay?" Jilly nodded, comforted.

Kit sat up. "So get that world-class body dressed. We're going to go over to the inn, and make coffee, and do the crossword puzzle, and maybe talk dirty to each other. And after the UPS man leaves I'm going to ravish you, in whatever room you want."

"Somewhere near the larder, of course," Jilly said, smiling at him as she pulled on her robe. "No contest."

"The larder it is," Kit said. "Last one dressed cooks breakfast."

KIT COOKED BREAKFAST, French toast loaded with powdered sugar and orange slices, while Jilly brewed the coffee. She started the crossword puzzle, and he browsed through the paper's business and sports sections. They ate huge breakfasts and talked lazily and laughed.

Finally Jilly pushed her empty plate away. "That was good. Kit," she said, "I've been meaning to ask you. Why didn't you go to Lavinia's funeral?"

Kit smiled at her over his half of the paper. "I expected to have to tell you earlier. I thought you would have asked me before we slept together."

Jilly toyed with her fork, feeling her cheeks redden. "I didn't want to know, because I wanted you so much I was out of my mind with it, and if you were an evil horrible creep who didn't really appreciate your wonderful grandmother and skipped her funeral for some dumb reason, I wouldn't be able to have you. This way, at least, I got to have you once."

"Twice, actually."

"Twice. Could you put me out of my misery here?"

Kit laughed. "I had to have my wisdom teeth out. All four at once. The appointment happened to be for the day after Lavinia died. I was miserable anyway, so I decided to get it over with. My face blew up like a balloon—a big fat black-and-blue balloon. I spent three days in my apartment in agony, sipping ginger ale through a straw, so zonked on painkillers I couldn't stand up."

"Oh." Jilly felt relieved and suddenly lighthearted. She felt her mouth begin to twitch. She coughed, trying to hide it.

"Agony. Did you hear me say I was in agony? This is just what I was afraid of, that you would laugh. It isn't funny, Jillian." Kit gave her hand a little smack.

"No. Of course not," Jilly said, trying valiantly to keep her face straight.

"And I'm sure you understand that it's embarrassing. I mean, no thirty-seven-year-old guy wants to lose it over a couple of stupid teeth."

"Yes. Of course." He was right. She should definitely not laugh. Despite herself, she could feel a giggle bubbling up in her throat. "I'm just...happy. Giddy. I was afraid it was something so much worse. And it's just...the picture of you, a guy as big and tough and handsome as you, all...lumpy and grumpy and...mumpy," she added, laughing. "Like a little kid. Did the tooth fairy leave you money? Did Hank read you bedtime stories?"

"That tears it." Kit tried not to laugh along with her. He was damned if he was going to encourage this kind of disrespect, and on the morning after a night during which he'd made her howl with pleasure, no less. "I am never telling you anything again." He stood up and began clearing the table, banging her breakfast plate down on top of his, dumping their silverware on top.

"Did you wear flannel pajamas with feet in them?" Jilly gasped, breathless with laughter.

"Never. I am never telling you anything again," he said over his shoulder as he strode toward the kitchen. "And I'm never having sex with you again, either."

"Oooh, his pride is hurt," Jilly called after him. "I'm so-o-o scared. No more sex, ever? Not even on special occasions, like the summer equinox or Christmas or—" Jilly cracked up again "—Abraham Lincoln's birthday?"

"At least not until noon. Where the hell is that UPS guy?" Kit said to himself in the kitchen, looking at his watch.

KIT WAS FINISHING THE breakfast dishes when the UPS man arrived. He wiped his hands on the back of his jeans and wandered to the front of the hotel. He watched with astonishment as twelve large cardboard boxes were unloaded from the truck.

"I thought you said they were just delivering pillows," he said, surveying the cartons stacked in the parlor.

"I did." Jilly handed him a knife. "Here, help me open these. You'll see."

Kit took the knife and set to work. Sure enough, the first box was filled with blue floral throw pillows piped in yellow, the second with rose-checked toss pillows, the third with needlepoint bolsters edged with rows of silky tassels. There were square pillows and round pillows, whimsical pillows and serious pillows. "Are you nuts, woman?" he said, watching her unpack still more pillows. "There are enough throw pillows here to furnish Pakistan, much less one little old hotel."

"Not that many, really. I know what I'm doing. Stick with the garden, boyo," Jilly said, lifting a pair of tapestry cushions from still another box.

"I'm serious." A frown creased Kit's forehead. "It's going to look like the inside of a girl's dorm."

"It is not. But for the record, what's so wrong with a girl's dorm? What would you prefer it to look like? A locker room? A pool hall? The poop deck of *H.M.S. Bounty?*"

"At least the *Bounty* wouldn't be ditsy," Kit said, looking down his nose at her, enchanted as always by her feistiness. "You do want men in this inn, I presume. Well, I really can't stand ditsy, and trust me, most men can't, either."

"Well, kiss my grits." Jilly batted her eyelashes at him. "What do you know. The elected representative of the red-blooded American male, right here on my l'il old premises. Let me just start makin' you feel at home, sugar. What should I do first? Order up a few Barcaloungers? Get out those big-screen TVs? Install magic-finger mattresses?"

"Sounds great," Kit said. "Don't forget the complimentary copies of *Penthouse, Popular Mechanics* and *Trout and Stream.*"

"You know, smarty, a few years ago there was a major study that showed that over 70 percent of men surveyed liked a flowery, feminine ambience in hotel bedrooms."

"Really?" Kit snorted, unimpressed. "What did their boyfriends think?"

"God, you're so unenlightened. I told you, Malone, stick to the garden. That's a big enough project for one man to ruin. You don't have to blight the interior of the place, too." As punctuation, Jilly picked up one of the pillows, gave it her best windup and threw it across the room. It hit Kit hard on the nose, then bounced off. "Meddling creep," she added with a grin, turning away from him in dismissal.

"Hostile man hater," Kit said, his face red. Picking up a

deep blue needlepoint bolster by its tasseled fringe, he gave her a resounding smack on her shapely denim-covered rear.

Startled, Jilly lost her balance, tripping over one stack of pillows and falling onto her knees in another. "Chauvinist pig," she grunted. Jumping to her feet, she grabbed a ruffled square and swung it at him two-handed.

"Bossy little spitfire," Kit gasped, grabbing the pillow's other end and starting to wrench it away.

"Don't rip my pillows...macho jerk." Swiftly, she hooked her sneakered foot behind his left calf and pulled. Unprepared for the move, he found his legs slipping out from under him and his rear hitting the floor with a jarring thump. "Damn it!" he cursed, flailing around for her ankles. "That was hitting below the belt," he complained, giving up. He propped himself up on his elbows and regarded her from the floor. It was novel, seeing her from this viewpoint. Even from below she still looked great.

"I would never, ever hit you below the belt, Malone," Jilly insisted breathlessly. Gracefully, she lowered herself onto his prone body, straddling his waist. "That area is way too valuable to me. Your head, however, is useless, and therefore fair game."

"Hellcat," he said.

"Yes. I won," she announced, sitting astride him, letting her full weight rest on his groin.

"Mmm," Kit said. "I let you."

"Liar."

"Cheat."

"It's so warm out, and that pillow fight didn't help. I need to cool down," Jilly complained, shifting on his thighs. Teasingly, she unbuttoned her Hawaiian-print camp shirt to reveal the lacy camisole beneath. The white of the camisole set off her smooth tan. Kit could see the rosy disks of her nipples through the fabric and a line of smooth flesh where it ended at her waist.

"Your underwear is going to kill me, woman," he groaned.

"Oh," Jilly said innocently. "Then, I guess it's a good thing I'm not wearing panties."

Kit blinked up at her. "You do know that a beautiful woman who doesn't wear underwear is every guy's secret fantasy?" he asked, his voice hoarse. "You wouldn't lie about a thing like that, would you?"

Smiling into his eyes, Jilly lifted her hips and slid down the zipper of her jeans. Craning his neck to look at her, Kit could see a triangle of bare flesh and the slightest wisp of curly golden-brown hair.

He groaned. "It's a huge sacrifice, but I've decided to lift my ban on sex."

"I was hoping you would." Jilly bent over and gave him a kiss. "Wanna go up to your room?"

"Too many dirty socks. Let's try yours." Kit stood up and took Jilly's hand to lead her up the stairs.

"I could get used to this," Jilly said, taking the steps two at a time.

"Me, too," Kit said, following her, his hand on her waist. "It's heaven."

"Heaven with too many throw pillows," Jilly said, straight-faced.

"I was probably wrong about them," Kit conceded. "Really, I was."

"Ha. You are so pathetically transparent," Jilly said as they reached her room. "You would agree with anything I said right now, just so that I'll make love with you."

"Yup. You're absolutely right. No argument from me," Kit said, and slammed her bedroom door behind them.

8

OVER THE NEXT DAY OR SO, Kit and Jilly settled into a comfortable routine. Their daily rhythms meshed perfectly. Kit worked on his stocks and the garden while Jilly managed the shop and made progress on the interior of Truelove House. Late one afternoon they snuck off to laze on the beautiful beach of Bahia Honda. They ate dinner with friends and spent an evening happily alone. They played volleyball. They went to bed early and made love a lot.

They talked lazily but constantly. Jilly told Kit about her parents and her life in Atlanta, the divorce, the early days of her shop. She didn't say very much about Claude, but Kit began to get the picture. Kit told Jilly about his family, his parents' deaths and his years at Yale.

"I can't quite figure out where the Kit who wore an earring fits, between an honors degree from Yale and a career as a stock-market wizard," Jilly said one afternoon as they worked on one of the inn's bedrooms. Jilly was perched on a ladder hanging a wallpaper border under the room's slanted eaves. Kit was handing her supplies, keeping her company and watching her work. She was wearing baggy white painter's pants and a little sleeveless cotton undershirt with lace around the neck. Her hair was messy and she was wearing no makeup. As always, he thought she looked great.

"Oh, that. My lost year." Kit dunked a strip of border in water, folded it into lengths, and handed it up to her.

Jilly took the wallpaper strip in her hands and leaned down toward him. "Why does a person's nose always start to itch just when her hands are covered with gooky junk? Could you scratch mine for me? What lost year?"

"My parents died in that car crash I told you about during my last year at Yale," Kit said, wiping his hands on the back of his jeans. He reached up and gently rubbed Jilly's nose. "Better? I made it through graduation, but I just couldn't face going on for my M.B.A. like I'd planned. I came down to see Lavinia instead. She was devastated, too, and we helped each other get through the summer. Finally, though, I think she got afraid I was hanging around because I felt obligated to take care of her. She called me a complete waste of my parents' educational dollars, and a self-pity junkie, and finally just a lazy bum. Ready for the next strip?"

"Yeah. Thanks. Keep talking."

"Yes, boss. I took off in this old VW bug and eventually ended up in California. I spent the whole year there, in Laguna Beach, hanging out, drinking beer and doing a little surfing."

"You? Hanging out? Is this crooked?" Jilly said, squinting at the latest line of border.

"No. Wait. Yes, but the line of the ceiling is crooked, too. The house must have settled."

"I want it to be right."

"It is right, as right as it can be."

"No. I want it to be *right*."

"Darling," Kit said, "this has been our first two consecutive days without a major argument and I hate to break the streak, but has anyone told you you have this little tendency to fixate on utterly ridiculous things?"

"Whereas you," Jilly told him as she climbed down the ladder, "concentrate on the big picture, the significant stuff. For example, yesterday, when you went into a three-hour funk, complete with foot stamping, because one lousy little stock went down three little points." She stood by the door and looked up at the border. "I'm doing that piece over. It's definitely crooked."

"The difference between your border, which is not crooked, and my stock, you airhead, is that my lousy little stock lost a bunch of clients' money. And for the record I was not stamping. My foot had fallen asleep."

"I see. And I suppose the string of curses you were muttering under your breath were just a little wake-up call."

Kit laughed out loud. "I forgot about those. All right, so I'm obsessive, too. Here, brush that section by the window again, it's still bubbly. Do you want to hear the end of my story or not?"

"Don't you dare stop. My breath is bated. You were up to the surfing part."

"Yeah. At first it was great. But then the guys I roomed with and I started to bicker, and I started to fight with Alicia, who was my old lady, as we called it then."

Jilly set her wallpaper brush down. "I remember that lovely term," she said, keeping her voice light. "What was she like?"

"Alicia? Long blond hair, slender, pretty, tanned. One of those floaty, fragile kind of girls. She wore those Indian dresses girls wore then and she liked music—she worked at the record store—and she drank a lot. An awful lot. It was one of the things we argued about."

Kit handed Jilly the final length of border and she began to smooth it around the top of the room's last window. "Almost done," she said casually. She glanced at his face, which had the same unhappy expression she'd noticed for a moment on the first night they'd made love. "Go on. I'm listening."

"I feel dumb telling you all this. But anyway, in the end things just turned sour. I got bored, and I hated sitting around all the time. And Alicia got out of control. When I tried to talk to her about the drinking she got furious. And then one night she got drunk and she fell off somebody's deck. She got hurt really badly. None of us had any insurance, or any savings, and everyone at the damned party was too drunk to be any help. It was a nightmare. I called Lavinia, for the first time in months. She wired me money and took the next plane out. She made sure Alicia was taken care of and helped me pack up. I flew back home with her and a few months later I started my business degree at Wharton, thereby transforming myself into the type A maniac and Miami man-about-town you know and love. End of story."

"No wonder you didn't welcome the thought of hanging around Key West." Jilly hopped off the ladder and started to clean up the wallpapering supplies. "All this laid-back beach atmosphere must have stirred up some bad memories."

"Yeah. And you stirred up memories, too, at least at first. I'd always felt so damned guilty about Alicia. I couldn't shake the thought that I should have saved her somehow, that I could have taken care of her better. After that I just didn't get involved with vulnerable, sensitive women. Hell, I didn't really get involved at all, until I met you."

Jilly put her arms around him. "I'm glad you told me. You're a nice guy, Malone."

Kit held her close. "Not to mention a fabulous lover."

"I bet you even remembered to pick up the tomatoes we need for lunch?"

"Well, hey," Kit said, "two out of three."

WHEN THE PHONE RANG Kit was contemplating Jilly's collarbone. It was late Tuesday night and they were tangled together on Jilly's sofa eating popcorn, ignoring an old movie on cable and fooling around.

"Don't answer that," Kit mumbled, his face buried in the warm fragrant skin of her neck. Ignoring him, Jilly stuck her arm over the back of the couch and groped around on the sofa table. "It's for you," she said.

"Malone here. What is it?" Kit barked into the phone. He rested the receiver on Jilly's shoulder and tried not to lose track of what he was doing, which was tasting the utterly delicious hollow of her throat. *After almost forty ignorant years I finally discover not just the erotic appeal of collarbones but a woman with a world-class set of them,* he thought, *and some idiot has to interrupt me.*

"Angus MacPherson called, you rude son of a bitch," Hank Weinstein said from Miami.

"Yes!" Kit yelled. Instinctively he swung his body into an upright position, butting Jilly on the chin in the process. He mouthed an apology, slung an arm around her shoulders and turned back to the phone.

"Score so far, Malone one, Weinstein zero," he crowed.

"Kit?" Even long-distance, Hank's disdain was obvious. "Does the word *childish* ring any bells with you?"

"I'll admit to being childish, but I'm also happy."

"I hate you when you're happy."

"You hate me when I'm right, and I always told you MacPherson would call." Kit settled his bare feet on the floor and ran a hand through his hair as he thought.

Beside him, Jilly pulled the neck of her sweatshirt up and tried to muster some enthusiasm. Her face felt warm, her lips were swollen, her throat tickled from his kisses and she had that tight hot feeling that touching Kit always gave her. *I'm happy for him, whatever it is. Really. Well, not re-*

ally, not right now. I'll be happy for him later, she promised herself guiltily. *Right after he finishes licking my neck.*

"When does he want to see us?" Kit searched the coffee table for something to write with.

"You. He wants to see you, alone. On Thursday, at eleven. At MacPherson headquarters, the Howard Building, in Naples—not the Miami office where we met him before."

"Don't worry, Hank," Kit said. "I can handle this."

"Don't teeter on the back legs of your chair. Don't argue about politics."

"I can handle it, Hank."

"Don't spit on him. Remember the Coles."

"I can handle that, too." Tucking his scribbled reminder in his pocket, Kit watched as Jilly gave up on him, extricating herself from his arms and plopping herself down in the armchair near the TV. "Don't you just love Hepburn and Tracy?" she said to the air. "What a duo."

"We're not finished. Don't go away, honey," Kit said after her.

"We are too finished, and don't call me honey," Hank said in bafflement. "Malone, you are out of your mind."

"WHAT DO YOU THINK?" Kit asked, holding a red-patterned tie against his white-shirted chest and scrutinizing himself in the mirror.

"It's a very nice tie," Jilly said from her perch on the window seat. They were in Jilly's room at Truelove House, early on the Thursday morning of Kit's appointment with Angus MacPherson.

"The red is bright and modern looking, which is good. Or maybe it's bad—maybe it's too aggressive for Angus MacPherson."

"Maybe," Jilly agreed, lost in dreamy contemplation of

the curve of his hips in his impeccably fitted gray worsted trousers. *He's perfect. Perfect shoulders, perfect waist, perfect rear. Particularly perfect rear. You never realize how many men have less than perfect rears until a Kit Malone wanders into your life. How can any human being be this beautiful?* she wondered. *It's indecent. Or maybe it's my obsession with him that's indecent. But if Mother Nature didn't want me to obsess, she shouldn't have given him that rear end.*

"The yellow is more conservative," Kit was saying, a clutch of ties in his hand, "but it's kind of blah. I don't want Angus MacPherson to view me as blah. But I don't want him to see me as overly brash, either. Damn it. I have the perfect tie for this meeting, a maroon Geoffrey Beene with little navy squiggles, but it's in Miami."

"Can't you stop off and buy a new one here?"

"Where do you suggest I find it? Elmer's House of Souvenirs or the Key West branch of T-Shirts 'R' Us?" Kit snapped.

"I beg your pardon...Beau Brummell," Jilly said.

Catching her eye in the mirror, Kit made a sheepish face. "I'm sorry. That was uncalled for."

Jilly curled her legs under her and tied her robe more tightly around her waist. "It's okay, Malone. But the truth is that it's just no use asking me about ties. I personally would let you manage every dime I owned even if your only tie had a picture of Elvis and sang the first line of 'Love Me Tender' every time you sneezed."

Kit leaned over to deposit a quick kiss on her mouth, then dropped onto the window seat beside her. "That besotted, huh?"

"Yup. But don't get uppity."

"No chance. I'm besotted, too. And the problem here isn't ties, anyway. The truth is that I just don't know what MacPherson wants. He knows our record. He's had our pitch. He's waiting for something else, and for the life of me I can't figure out what it is. What the hell have I missed?"

Jilly straightened his collar and brushed a stray lock of black hair off his neck. "What was your first meeting like? Were you charming to him?"

"Of course," Kit told her, raising his eyebrows. "I ooze charm. It's a reflex. Haven't you noticed?"

"Not exactly," Jilly said, and they laughed together. "Are you nervous?"

"Nah," Kit said. "Well, a little. Sort of. Completely. I really want this account."

"I wish I could help. But anyway, you'll do fine."

"Want to come?" Kit, suddenly busy with his cuff links, kept his voice casual.

"Anytime, and always," Jilly said, deadpan.

"I don't mean that, not that I'm not agreeable. I mean to Naples. With me. You could keep me company on the ride and do some antiquing while I'm up in the Howard Building screwing up with Angus MacPherson."

I have a million things to do, Jilly thought. *We're independent beings with separate lives. I'm not his sidekick. Then again, he's beautiful, and I love him, and he's nervous enough to admit he's nervous, which means he's really, really nervous. I can do everything else tomorrow.* "I'd love to," she said. "Do I have to dress up?"

"Just enough so that I can take you someplace nice for lunch."

"Heels?"

"No heels. And no stockings. Please, no stockings. I have to concentrate. You could wear the dress you had on the day I met you, you know, the one with the big yellow buttons."

"Why? It's not sexy enough to distract you?" Jilly frowned.

"Are you kidding? I fantasized about those buttons for two solid weeks. I just figure I might have built up some immunity to that dress by now, whereas with something new, who knows?"

"We'll see," Jilly said. "Out of my way, I have to get dressed. In something suitably undistracting. Maybe I have a nun's habit lying around."

"Won't work. I've already considered the possibility, so I know. Meet you downstairs in a half hour?"

"Less," Jilly said. "And by the way...wear the red tie. Brash may be a problem, but blah just isn't you."

"Mr. Malone. Nice to see you," Angus MacPherson said. "Coffee?"

Kit sat in Angus MacPherson's office trying not to sweat. Trying not to teeter on the back legs of his chair. Trying not to screw up. If he screwed up with Angus MacPherson after all the bragging he'd done to Hank, he'd have to flee the country.

Which would be fine, actually, he thought. *I bet Jilly would like, say, Tahiti more than she likes Miami.*

"Yes, sir, thank you. Black is fine." While Angus Mac-Pherson poured the coffee himself, from a carafe on the credenza behind his desk, Kit took a moment to regroup. Angus MacPherson rattled him. Unlike most clients, Angus didn't act tough or hostile. He was full of down-home gestures, like pouring the coffee himself rather than calling some minion to do it. Maybe that was the problem, Kit thought. The guy had built a multimillion-dollar conglomerate out of virtually nothing. How could he seem so nice? It just had to be a ploy.

"Here you are. So, Mr. Malone," Angus said, sitting in the armchair across from Kit.

"Yes, Mr. MacPherson," Kit said.

"I know about your investment style. Tell me something about your life. What you like, what you do in your spare time, what you hope to accomplish. Not because I'm nosy, you understand, although—" Angus's eyes sparkled "—my competitors would say that I'm very nosy indeed. But because I believe that the best business relationships are built between people who view the world in similar or at least compatible ways."

Kit looked at him, nonplussed. His mind raced. Swiftly he decided that honesty was the best, the only course. Maybe. Angus MacPherson looked steadily at him. "A few months back, I could have answered that easily," Kit began. "I would have told you about my business, which I love, and my life in Biscayne Bay, and my grandmother, who was pretty much what I had of family until she died this summer."

Angus took a sip of his coffee. "But?"

Kit paused. *If I lie, I'm going to sound insincere. If I'm honest, I'm going to sound like a dope. I'm gonna have to be honest, but please, whoever is in charge of these things, don't let me lose this account because I sound like John-Boy Walton,* he prayed. "I met a woman, actually," he said.

"Ah," said Angus MacPherson.

"I met a woman who matters to me. I didn't want to get involved with her, and she's not even the kind of woman I thought I'd like, but she's totally changed my life. I'm like a different person."

"Different?"

"Alive," Kit said.

"And what are your plans?"

"I want to marry her." Feeling incredibly stupid, Kit

paused. *This is beginning to sound like Ann Landers,* he thought. "But she's very independent, and our lives don't entirely mesh. I'm not sure what will actually happen. I've learned that with Jilly it's best not to take anything for granted."

"She's unpredictable?" Angus asked.

"As lightning, sir," Kit said. "Also smart and stubborn."

"My Anna was like that. Kept me guessing for thirty-nine years. It's healthy for a man, having a strong woman to balance him. Did this young woman accompany you today?"

"Uh, yes." Kit paused, wary, not sure where this was going. "She's going to meet me downstairs, for lunch."

Angus MacPherson stood. "Perhaps the two of you will lunch with me. In our corporate dining room at, say, twelve?"

"Gladly, sir," Kit said faintly. Imagining his impetuous, fast-talking, businessman-hating Jilly chatting over fillet of sole with Angus MacPherson, Kit kissed this client goodbye.

JILLY SHOOK ANGUS MacPherson's hand and fell in love. If a genie ever offered to deliver up the father of her dreams, this would be the man she would order—a complete contrast to her own tall, thin, fussy, formal parent. Angus MacPherson was a lived-in man.... That was the only phrase Jilly could find to describe him. Around sixty or so, he had iron gray hair styled in a rough crew cut, a big beaky nose and a face creased with the lines of a lot of tough living. His light blue eyes were shrewd but not, she sensed, without the capacity to twinkle. Angus MacPherson exuded power, but Jilly found him somehow comforting. She smiled up at him fearlessly and returned his strong handshake with vigor.

In the MacPherson Corporation's private dining room they were served tall frosty glasses of iced tea and plates of crisp salad. Jilly nibbled while she gazed around the room. It was an impressive place with gray silk-lined walls and Ansel Adams photographs, but it was somehow wrong. As Kit and Angus chatted about long-term trends in government bonds, she mentally rearranged it.

"Kit here tells me you're an interior decorator," Angus said, breaking into her reverie.

"Yes, that's true," Jilly said.

"What do you think of this room?"

"I don't understand it," she said without thinking.

Angus MacPherson's eyes gleamed. Giving Jilly a panicked stare, Kit dropped his fork onto the floor. Silently he bent to pick it up. When his face emerged from below the table it was studiously impassive.

Jilly darted a quick apologetic glance in his direction.

Good girl, Jillian, she thought despairingly. *He's worked on this account for months, and you're going to kill it arguing about carpet colors.*

"What is it you don't understand?" Angus asked.

If I lie, Jilly thought, *I'm going to sound insincere. If I'm honest, I'm going to sound like a know-it-all. I'm gonna have to be honest, but please, whoever is in charge of these things, don't let me lose him this account because I sound like Martha Stewart,* she prayed.

"It's a beautiful room," she said truthfully. "Very impressive."

"But?" Angus probed. Kit chewed his grilled tuna steak and gave her the sickly smile of a man condemned to die.

"Well, who eats here?" she continued, warming to her theme despite her better judgment. "Friends and colleagues, whom you want to relax so that you can cement your relationships with them. And enemies, whom you want to relax so that they'll let their defenses down. Either way, relaxation is key. And this room isn't relaxing."

"Is your fish all right, Mr. Malone?" Angus reached for a roll.

"Great," Kit mumbled, chewing manfully on what tasted like expensive sawdust.

"Please don't stop now, Ms. Sanderson," Angus said.

Jilly took a deep breath. "This room puts me on my guard. The gray is sterile, the furniture is severe and the light from those fixtures makes both of you look like you haven't slept for weeks."

"I haven't, thanks to you," Kit muttered under his breath.

"Excuse me?" Angus said.

"Nothing. Excellent baby squash," Kit answered grimly.

Angus took a sip of his tea. "An interesting point, Ms. Sanderson—or may I call you Jillian? What would you change?" he asked. Jilly glanced in Kit's direction. He made a small flapping motion of surrender.

"I would leave the drapes, the carpeting and most of the furniture just the same," she said. "All I would change is the mood. People relax in warm colors, soft textures, flattering light. I would redo the walls in a more inviting color...an ivory, maybe, or moss green or a terra-cotta shade. I would cushion these chairs and use lamps with fabric shades to give a warmer, more flattering light. I would put flowers on the sideboard and move those photographs to another place. They're gorgeous, but they're too severe. I would find something big and dramatic, full of life and color, instead. One of those huge Audubon prints of predatory birds might be appropriate," she finished teasingly, going for broke.

"You know, I've always thought this place looked like a

morgue. Perhaps you would take on the project for me?"
Angus said.

"No," Jilly answered. Red-faced, Kit dropped his fork
again.

"May I ask why not?"

"Diagnosing a problem is easy, Mr. MacPherson. Actually curing it is something else. The best people to fix this
room are the people who decorated it in the first place. Tell
them what we talked about today. They'll get the idea. As
for me, well, if you ever have a regular old ordinary family
dining room to redecorate, I'm your girl."

"I do, as a matter of fact," Angus said. "Since my wife
died a few years ago, my children and grandchildren tell
me the house looks sad and faded. Perhaps you'd like to
come over and take a look some weekend."

"I'd love to."

"One final question, then," Angus MacPherson said.
"What do you think of Christopher, here?"

Jilly thought for a moment. "I think he's a very good
person," she said.

"Ah." Angus MacPherson smiled. "I hope you're not
saying that under his brilliant and very aggressive exterior
beats the heart of a teddy bear."

"No. That would be a lie. I'm just saying that under his
brilliant and very aggressive exterior beats a heart."

"Yes. That's helpful," Angus said. "So, Christopher. I'll
try you with seventy million to start, and we'll proceed
from there. If you speak to Melissa in my office tomorrow,
she'll get the paperwork started."

"Thank you, Mr. MacPherson," Kit said. "I'll do a good
job with it."

"Angus, please. I expect you will. Goodbye, Christopher. Goodbye, Jillian."

"Goodbye, Angus," Jilly said, beaming up at him.

Angus MacPherson's eyes twinkled.

"I CAN'T THANK YOU ENOUGH. I'm forever in your debt," Kit said, stopping so that Jilly could precede him through the Howard Building's revolving door. "And if you ever, ever do anything like that again I'm going to shave your cat."

"I'm sorry, Kit," Jilly said, reaching for his hand as they stepped out onto the heat of the city sidewalk. "I truly am. It just happened, I didn't plan it."

"I know that, dummy. That's what's so scary."

"Did you really keep dropping your fork, or was that just an excuse to hide your face?"

"I kept dropping my fork. My palms were sweaty with terror."

Jilly squeezed his hand. "I can't believe you're this insecure. I knew you had him from the moment I met him."

"Sure."

"Kit," she said reasonably, "someone who's not going to hire you doesn't ask to meet your girlfriend."

"That's true, I suppose," Kit allowed.

"Which reminds me. What exactly did you tell him about me?"

"I'm taking the Fifth on that," Kit said. "It was between us men."

Jilly stopped under the awning of a fancy woman's shop. "Kit, where are we going?"

"I have no idea. Do you want to browse around some more and then have dinner here?"

Jilly tilted her head, considering. "To tell you the truth, I've had enough civilization for one day. I'd personally like to go home, change into jeans and have dinner at Ernest's. We can buy the guys a beer to celebrate your new account."

"Don't say that word. I'm off beer for life. But I'm happy to go home. Your wish is my command."

"Sure," Jilly scoffed. "And the Dalai Lama wears in-line skates."

"Well, sometimes," Kit said. "Your wish is my command sometimes."

"Wrong again. My wish is your command whenever it happens to match up exactly with what you want to do anyway. Give it up, Malone. Just lead me to the car. I've had enough city life to last me for months."

How about a trip to Miami next Thursday? Kit asked her silently, thinking guiltily of his promise to Hank. Six more days, he counted, and shivered. Somehow, despite all their time together, he hadn't mentioned his need to return to work to Jilly and Jilly hadn't asked. He could fake it for a while, he knew, work during the week and come and see her on the weekends. But it wasn't a solution. He didn't want to have to miss her four nights a week, but she obviously didn't want to live in Miami. *God knows, she's been clear enough on that score,* he thought. And suddenly the euphoria of the afternoon was touched by a shiver of fear.

THE JOLTING OF THE car woke Jilly.

"Where are we?" she asked, disoriented.

"Deer Key, honey," Kit said. "You had a nice long nap."

"Mmm. I'm sorry, Kit. You must have been bored."

Kit kept his eyes on the tricky curve of road ahead, but she could see the side of his mouth quirk mischievously upward. "Not exactly," he said. "You look very sexy when you sleep."

"I felt very sexy," Jilly said. She'd been having a dream in which she and Kit had great sex on the front seat of the Jaguar. In dreams, impediments like stick shifts and the curious eyes of other drivers didn't exist. In her dream their coupling was graceful and easy and hot. Her cheeks flushed. "Actually," she added timidly, "I *feel* very sexy."

Kit turned his head to look at her, making the car swerve. He straightened it, then leaned to touch her knee. "Luckily, it's not that far to Key West," he said.

"Yeah." Jilly straightened in her seat, pulling her dress down over her knees. She smiled briefly, but secretly his sensible reaction depressed her. *Grow up, Sanderson,* she thought. *The fact that you've discovered the joy of sex so recently doesn't mean that he has. Unlike you, he's probably actually had some orgasms in the past ten years.* He had just driven for hours and won a major client. He was thirty-seven, not sixteen. What had she expected? That he would reach his hand under the hem of her sundress and caress her bare thigh? Lean over at the next stoplight and kiss her passionately? Be so overcome with desire he would pull off the road into some sleazy motel?

A minute later, Kit pulled the car off the road, bringing the Jaguar's powerful engine to a swift silent halt under a blinking neon Island Motor Court. Vacancy sign. He shut off the car and turned to Jilly, lifting her chin with his finger and giving her a swift hard kiss. "Lock the door after me and stay right here, lady," he told her. "I'll be right back."

Wide-eyed, Jilly could only nod.

Three minutes later, Kit returned with a small key on a plastic chain. He helped Jilly out of the Jaguar, opened the door and led her into the small dim room. Jilly began to speak, but he stopped her, putting his fingers on her lips. "No," he whispered. "Let me do this."

In the corner of the room stood a scarred walnut highboy. Kit lifted Jilly's hands, bracing them a foot or so apart on the dresser top, and turned her so that she was standing with her back to the room. She heard him shrugging out of his jacket and tossing it on the bed. He stood behind her and suddenly his big strong knowing hands were on her breasts, circling them, stroking them hard. It was the first time their lovemaking hadn't started slowly, with tenderness and kisses, and it was so *good*, Jilly thought, excited by the directness of him, the controlled roughness with which he touched her breasts and then moved lower, stroking her through her sundress, reaching between her thighs, never stopping.

She was so hot, Kit marveled, his heart pounding like a jackhammer, so flushed with drowsiness and desire. Suddenly he couldn't wait, but she was so ready he didn't need to. He pulled up her sundress with one hand, loving the silky feel of her skin under the crisp cotton, and yanked at his clothes with the other. He let her go, to fumble with the foil packet he'd tucked in his pocket that morning just in case. Then he took hold of her again, angling his thigh between hers, lifting her, slipping inside her wetness from behind, his arm underneath her breasts, his mouth kissing her neck and cheek, her body arched against him, riding him.

I would die for him. This is craziness, Jilly thought, bucking against him.

Don't let me lose her, this is love, Kit thought, taking her, possessing her, surrendering to her, not just his body but his soul.

Afterward Kit held Jilly on his lap, rocking her, then kissed the top of her head. "You okay to leave now? I don't want you to feel rushed, but this place doesn't feel very secure."

Jilly lifted her head. "No, I guess not," she said, smiling. "Can you believe I didn't notice?"

"I'm going take it as a compliment."

"You should." Ruefully, Jilly pulled at her sticky,

creased sundress. She glanced at herself in the motel's spotted mirror. She looked rumpled, drained, flushed and happy.

Any moron could tell you've just had sex, Jilly, she thought. *Any moron could tell you've just had great sex.*

"Is there any point in trying to shower here," she said, giving up. "Or should we just go home?"

"Let's just drive. We can take a long, deep bath together back at the inn. I've been wanting to check out one of those claw-footed tubs. Besides," Kit grinned, "I like the way you smell."

Jilly nodded and slipped her feet into her shoes. "Let's hit the road, then. Do you think we'll be able to sneak into Truelove House without bumping into anyone we know?"

"Probably. But if not, to hell with them," Kit said. "I'm not ashamed of anything we've done. Are you?"

"God, yes." Jilly laughed, remembering their feverish coupling. "But please don't let that stop you."

TWO HOURS LATER, the Jaguar turned off Duval Street.

"Home sweet hotel, here we come," Kit said. "The inn looks good from a distance, don't you think? Even with the garden only half finished. But who are those goons on the porch?"

"Hellfire and damnation," Jilly breathed. "One of those goons is Claude."

"Claude?" Kit said, confused. "Oh, no. *The* Claude?"

"The very one," said Jilly grimly. "I have no idea who the other one is."

"I do." Kit made a face as the car pulled closer to the inn. "It's Hank. Henry Weinstein, my partner, come no doubt to find out if I screwed up with Angus MacPherson."

"Maybe it's not too late to turn around. Maybe they haven't seen us," Jilly said.

"Too late. Hank can pick this car out from two miles away, and it looks like Claude's seen you."

"Well, onward, then. Ours is not to question why, ours is just to do or die."

"Damn," Kit said.

"Damn. Double damn. Damn squared," Jilly said. "Damn to the max."

9

"STAY OUT OF THIS," Jilly said, taking a quick look at her face in the rearview mirror. "Ugh. I look horrible."

"You look gorgeous, Jilly," Kit began.

"Stay out of it, Kit." Jilly unbuckled her seat belt and tugged her sundress over her knees. Despite the tension of the moment, Kit smiled. "I know you feel protective," she insisted. "But go talk to your partner and leave Claude alone."

"Why? He's just going to hurt you. If he hurts you, I'll want to kill him anyway. Might as well get it over with."

"Malone." Jilly raised her chin and turned to face him. "Listen to me. Now."

Kit hadn't seen her eyes flash like that since that first day, in her shop. He'd lost that battle and he sensed he was about to lose this one, but he still didn't want to give in. He propped one arm on the Jaguar's steering wheel and regarded Jilly stubbornly.

"Malone," she said again. "I've run away from Claude for years. I can't do it anymore. I have to do this by myself. I understand that your caveman instincts are going crazy and you'd like nothing better than to come on in and beat the bejesus out of the guy, but you need to understand that you can't."

"Fine. You're probably right. Maybe. You have fifteen minutes," Kit said mulishly.

"That's ridiculous. God knows I don't want to sit

around chatting with him, but maybe there's business to be discussed. Thirty."

"Twenty. That's final."

Jilly lifted her handbag and sandals from the floor of the car. "Sometimes you make me want to scream."

"Good. That's healthy. Scream at Claude." He reached over her and unlatched the door. "Go ahead, Wonder Woman, strut your stuff."

KIT ANGLED THE JAGUAR into a curbside parking space and met Hank on the sidewalk.

"Henry. Come to check on me?" Kit said without enthusiasm, watching over Hank's head as Jilly led Claude through the inn's front door.

"Absolutely. I had to pick up some paperwork from a client in Key Largo, so I thought I'd drop by." Hank craned his neck. "Who is that guy?"

"Jilly's ex-husband, Claude." Abruptly Kit turned and gestured toward the back of the inn. "Come on, let's go get something cold to drink."

"She doesn't look happy to see him," Hank said, following after Kit.

"She's not." In the kitchen, Kit handed Hank a can of beer and took a can of cola for himself. Moodily he propped his hips against the kitchen counter. "He's a creep, to put it mildly."

"Oh." Hank took a deep swig from his can. "That hits the spot. Route 1 is a killer. So what happened with MacPherson?"

"Seventy million to start, more later—assuming we don't screw it up. You can do the paperwork on Monday," Kit said absently.

"I've got to hand it to you, jerk though you are," Hank marveled. "That's fabulous. Just think of the commissions, not to mention the prestige. I never thought you could pull it off. What did you do to convince him?"

"I told him about Jilly, and Jilly told him his company dining room was decorated all wrong. He loved it, for some reason," Kit said. "The question is, what to do about him?"

"MacPherson? What else is there to do? We're golden."

"Henderson. Claude Henderson, you fool."

"I don't get it. I never get it with you anymore."

"She wants me to stay out of it, and I will, for her damned fifteen minutes," Kit reflected aloud, ignoring Hank's confusion. "But that bastard Claude is as slick as they come. He could surgically remove her heart and she'd never see the scalpel." Suddenly he snapped his fingers. "Yeah...that's a thought. And it won't even create a scene. Perfect."

"I'm lost," Hank said.

"Listen, Hank. We'll have dinner tonight—with Jilly, if she'll come. At, say, seven. Come back here." Kit tossed his soda can in the trash. "Right now, I need to go get ready."

"Ready? For what?" Hank shook his head. "Really, I'm lost."

"Do a little sightseeing," Kit said, patting Hank on the shoulder as he headed for the stairs. "Go see the lighthouse or the Truman summer White House. Really, you'll enjoy it. Key West is a fabulous place."

HER FACE CALM, Jilly watched Claude talk. It was a horrible but fascinating experience, kind of like watching yourself fall off a cliff in slow motion.

Claude sounded exactly the same. His voice was still thin and slightly nasal and he pronounced his words precisely, as if he were not so much talking as enunciating. He still wagged his right index finger in the air when he wanted to emphasize a point, as though she were a slow learner who needed visual aids. He looked the same, too. Maybe a bit balder than he had been four years ago—his forehead seemed to end only a few inches above the back of his neck—but his face was still full and handsome, in a bland way. He still wore a navy blazer and a Rolex and the gold signet ring Jilly had always hated. And to her astonishment, he still wanted to be married to her. Or so he said. Because the sense of subtle manipulation was the same, too.

Claude is the same, Jilly thought. *It must be me that's changed.* Eight years ago, she had married Claude and meant it. She had never loved him the way she loved Kit, but she had respected him, wanted to make him a home. Tried to please him and grew worried when she didn't, which was often. She'd made him the center of her world, so that his opinions colored everything she felt.

Now she looked at Claude and felt as numb as if someone had shot novocaine into her soul. She guessed she should be glad that the pain and humiliation of her marriage were over. Instead, she simply felt the same way Claude had so often made her feel. Depressed. Apathetic. Dead. How had she chosen to spend her life with this inadequate, heartless man?

Is this how I'm going to feel about Kit in ten years? she wondered. *Am I going to look at his face and feel so empty I could cry?*

She nodded when Claude seemed to expect it, and thought about Kit—about the fury she felt at his dumb opinions, the tenderness she felt when he looked vulnerable, the joy she felt when they laughed together, the heat she felt when he kissed her and stroked her and rocked her underneath him.

No, she decided. *In the absolute worst case, in ten years I'm going to look at Kit Malone's face and feel like belting him one in the jaw. And if things go well, I'm going to look at him and still want to rip his clothes off.* And as she began to explain that it was absolutely, utterly out of the question that she go back to Claude, she managed to smile a tiny, secret, almost invisible smile.

PRECISELY SEVENTEEN minutes after Jilly led Claude into the parlor, the door swung open and Kit breezed into the room. He was wearing his fancy suit, now with the blah yellow tie. His hair was damp and combed straight back from his face, the usual wild tumble subdued into military precision with what smelled like styling mousse. He wore a moist rosebud in his buttonhole.

At least the roots don't show, Jilly thought, trying to mask her bewilderment.

"Sorry, darling," he said. "Oh, my apologies. I didn't realize you had someone here."

Jilly stared at him, mesmerized. He sounded like a commentator for the BBC, sort of nasal and affected. What in the world was he doing? With an effort, she tried to be polite. "Um. Claude Henderson, Christopher Malone. Kit, my ex-husband, Claude."

Kit pumped Claude's hand enthusiastically. Claude was five inches shorter than he was. He stood up straight to emphasize the difference. From that vantage point, he could see that Claude was quickly going bald. *Serves you right, you disgrace to American manhood,* he thought. *I hope your shiny white teeth fall out, too.*

"F. Claude Henderson? Well! I'm honored to finally meet you. I believe one of my clients, Chad Pitt-Kelton, is a friend of yours. Lovely guy, Chad, and I'm pleased to say we've made him a bundle in the options market. And let me see...was it Biff Pierrpont at Windsor Polo who knows you? No? Someone else," Kit lied blithely. "I'd love to chat, we must have so many friends in common, but Jilly and I have dinner and the opera to get to. You know how it is."

"Opera?" Claude Henderson said, glancing at Jilly, who nodded pleasantly, exactly like she knew what Kit was babbling about.

"Pavarotti," Kit said. "At the Key Largo Playhouse. Iffy acoustics, of course, and naturally he hasn't been in truly superb voice since the '89 season. Still, people as fortunate as we are must do what we can to support local culture, don't you agree? And Jilly here is the backbone of their fund-raising committee. Mrs. Parrish—you know, Claude, the Winston Parrishes, such marvelous people, even if young Max did marry that vulgar Italian contessa—was singing her praises at the tennis club just the other day. And speaking of which...Jilly, darling?"

Jilly just looked at him, wide-eyed.

Kit moved his cuff to check his watch, then took her arm with a clasp considerably stronger than it looked. "I hate to rush you, honey, but you'll need to change pretty quickly. Rosita said to tell you that she made the fruit compote you wanted for breakfast and she picked up your black dress from the cleaner's. Hurry up, there's a darling." Holding the parlor door open he ushered her out, giving her a patronizing little smack on the rear in the process.

Once she was out of Claude's line of vision, he put his hand in the middle of her back and shoved. She wheeled around to glare at him. "Are you out of your mind?" she whispered.

"Wine? Of course I got the wine, darling," Kit said loudly, grinning at her. "A nice little white. Unpretentious but appealing. CeeCee will love it. Now run upstairs and don't worry your silly little head about anything but putting on that sexy dress of yours."

He stepped back into the parlor, smiling his best slick blindingly insincere corporate smile. "Women. You have to love 'em, right? Now, Claude. Can I get you a quick drink before we run? No? If you didn't bring a car, we'll be happy to drop you somewhere on our way—the Jaguar is a little tight, but we're all family, right?"

Claude gaped at him. "No, thank you, I have a driver. I need to be going, anyway. Do the two of you live here?"

Kit gave a hearty chuckle. "Of course not, old man. This was my grandmother's inn—Lavinia Stanton Malone, of the Boston branch of the family. Just a quick overnighter while our roof is being replaced. Actually, we divide our time between the cottage here and the penthouse in Biscayne. And then of course there's the condo in Aspen, but that hardly counts."

"May I ask how long you and Jillian have been...together?

"Oh, long enough, Claude, long enough," Kit said, guiding him out the front door with a firm hand. "Sometimes things don't work out between couples, we all know that. But between you and me, old man, you lost a real gem when you let that little lady go."

KIT BOUNDED UP THE stairs of the inn, taking the steps three at a time. He felt like a medieval knight who has just defended his castle and saved his princess from a nasty bout of barbarian pillage and rape.

"Bad news, Jillian, my pet," he said, arriving in her room. "Pavarotti had to cancel. Such a blow to local culture."

Jilly was sitting on her bed, arms clasped around her

knees. She looked at him expressionlessly. "You are completely nuts."

"When it comes to F. Claude Henderson you're the one who's nuts," Kit said.

"Me? I didn't invent an entire life on the spur of the moment. What did I do?"

"You let that worthless excuse for a man abuse you for almost twenty minutes and you did absolutely nothing to stop him."

"He wasn't abusing me. Well, not exactly."

"I was watching you. You looked like a deer caught in car headlights. You could have fought back. You could have called me."

"I could not have called you. It's my problem. I can't burden you with Claude."

"Sanderson," Kit said, sitting next to her and taking her hand, "I hate to break this to you, but you have already burdened me with Claude, just like I've burdened you with Alicia. That's what love is, having to pay the price for someone else's yucky past."

Jilly avoided his eye, her hand limp in his. "Maybe you're right, Kit. Look, I don't want to hurt your feelings, but I just need to be alone right now."

"No, you don't." Kit willed her to listen and she did, barely. "You've always been alone with this, really. I know it seems natural, but it's wrong. What you need to do right now is tell me exactly what that guy did to you."

Jilly shifted restlessly. "I don't like to talk about it."

"All right. But I need to hear about it."

Jilly stared down at her hands. "It's just so hard to explain. It sounds stupid, really. He didn't hit me, or mistreat me. He didn't even yell at me or anything. He just...chipped away at me. Everything I did was just a little bit wrong, and he always told me so, for my own good."

Jilly imitated Claude's thin voice. "'Perhaps a bit more makeup, Jillian, we wouldn't want the Morgans to think you're ill.' 'What a whimsical little dress, Jillian. Did you buy it on sale?' When I said something he didn't like in public, he did the same thing. 'That's our Jillian, so impulsive,' he'd say, and his friends would look at me with pity, like I was a disappointing child. He even did it in bed. Or he'd just go silent, so I knew I'd failed even though I didn't know at what."

"It doesn't sound stupid. It sounds controlling, sadistic and generally horrible," Kit said.

"I can see that now, I guess. But for a long time I didn't. I was used to being criticized. It seemed more or less normal. I guess I should have fought back, but I couldn't. I just got more tired and more timid and more hopeless. At least with you I know when I'm mad." Jilly squeezed Kit's hand. "Which is most of the time, of course."

"What did he want? Why did he come here today?" Kit asked.

"You won't believe it. At least, I didn't. He's moving to New York for a fancy new job. Suddenly he needs a wife and hostess, and I guess I was the easiest solution. He honestly thought I'd be grateful for his forgiveness, and excited about the prospect of entertaining his cronies from a Park Avenue penthouse."

"I hope you told him where to go."

"Of course. Well, I started to, but then this bozo in Gucci loafers breezed in."

"Come here." Kit held out his arms and gathered Jilly into them. She put her head on his shoulder, and he could feel her smile against his neck.

"Well, you certainly did cook Claude's goose," she admitted. "Imagine, his inadequate old Jillian already taken, by somebody just as rich, just as pretentious and twice as handsome as he is. Someone with a full head of hair, no less. But...Biff Pierrpont? Pavarotti? CeeCee? Rosita, the faithful maid? Really."

"Hush," he said. "Sometimes a guy's just gotta stand tall on his ramparts and let the burning arrows fall where they may."

"Please don't explain that to me," Jilly said, shaking her head. "I don't think I really want to know."

KIT, JILLY AND HENRY had dinner together at Chalfont's. Kit was pleased to see that Hank and Jilly got along fine. It was hard enough dealing with the two of them as it was. If they hated each other, life wouldn't be worth living.

Kit dropped Jilly off at her house and walked Hank to his car. "Congratulations," Hank said. "I really like her, Malone. You've done much better than I expected. So what's it like? You know."

"Like?" Kit looked at his friend, amused. "You wouldn't be asking about our sex life, would you? Because it would be incredibly vulgar and inappropriate for me to discuss that with you."

Hank grinned. "Of course."

"Fabulous," Kit said. "The best."

"Seriously, Kit. This Key West thing, which is driving me crazy, is it worth it?"

"Totally." Kit strolled down the street and looked up at the huge yellow moon and smiled to himself. "It's not just the sex, it's everything. It's just...great."

"When you get back to Miami, you'll have to bring her over to Brenda's."

"Yeah. You know, you and I have never done couple stuff together. I wonder why."

"Your other relationships lasted ten minutes apiece, you idiot," Hank said practically. "We'd all have time to grab a hot dog together, maybe, then boom. Your chick would be history."

Together the men walked to Hank's car, which was parked under a tree. "Well, I'm gonna want Jilly forever. The question is how to fix the fact that she hates where I live and I can't do business where she lives."

"But you're coming back to Miami on the fourth, anyway. Right, Malone?"

Kit looked at his partner's round, somewhat careworn face. He noticed the lines on Hank's forehead and the worry Hank was trying to suppress. *Hank has been good to me,* he acknowledged silently. *He's a nudge of the first magnitude, but he's good to me.* "The fourth. Can't wait. Right, boss," he said aloud. Kit waved as Hank drove away, a casual, confident, happy wave, exactly like a man who has his life figured out.

BELLE AND JILLY WERE in Belle's dining room, making goody bags for the boys' birthday party the next day. "It's chaos, I know," Belle said sheepishly, looking around the room.

"I like it." Jilly smiled. "It's nice."

"Maybe that means you're ready to have kids of your own."

"I don't like it *that* much," Jilly said hastily, "but time will tell."

Belle peeled open a caramel candy and popped it in her mouth. "What's it like with Kit? You know."

"I hope you're not expecting me to discuss what we do in B-E-D," Jilly said, keeping her voice low so that Belle's little girls, who were playing nearby, wouldn't hear her. "Because it would be truly crude for me to discuss something as private as that."

"B-E-D spells bed," Olivia Lincoln piped up from the doorway. Guiltily Jilly rolled her eyes.

"Thank you, honey. And C-A-T spells cat, right? You're so smart." Grinning, Belle handed her daughter four cookies. "Could you take these outside and share them with the other kids? You can play a while on the swings. Thanks, sweetie." She turned to Jilly. "As for asking you about you-know-what, I'm a mature woman, not a giggling teenager. I wouldn't dream of delving into your personal life."

"Uh-huh. What does F-A-B-U-L-O-U-S spell?"

"I knew it," said Belle, taking a cookie from the jar and handing one to Jilly.

"God, Belle, he's so smart and fun and sexy. He comes across like Mussolini, if Mussolini were dressed by Ralph Lauren, but really he's just so tender. So considerate."

"I want to be maid of honor, or whatever you call it, at the wedding."

"I think matron of honor is the term used for people who could actually give birth on or around the wedding day," Jilly said. "But I don't know his intentions, exactly, and anyway we would have a few logistical details to work out."

"When is he going back to Miami?"

"I don't know." Jilly tied a red bow around the final goody bag, then propped her chin in her hands. "We haven't talked about it. It's just about the only thing we haven't talked about, actually."

Belle piled the party favors in a cardboard box and reached for another cookie. Jilly grabbed her wrist and put it back. "Stop it," she said.

"It's sick, this craving for food." Belle sighed. "Why haven't you talked about it?"

"I don't know. It's silly. I guess I thought he'd mention it, ask me to come see his apartment or something, but he didn't. And now I can't figure out how to introduce the subject naturally."

"You really should talk about it," Belle said.

"I'll ask him. I will. Definitely. Any day now."

"I keep forgetting," Belle said, "Linc wants to know if you two want to come to dinner on Sunday."

"Sure. It'll be fun. What does Linc think about the new baby, or babies, as the case may be?" Jilly asked.

Belle made a face. "We haven't actually discussed it."

"You haven't *discussed* it?"

"He's got this huge presentation to give to the board of his company on Friday. I didn't want to freak him out until it's over."

"Hasn't he noticed that you're eating enough to nourish the population of Rhode Island?"

Belle stood up, smoothing her turquoise cotton smock over her still-flat stomach. "I don't snack in front of him. My waist is still more or less the same size, and I haven't had any morning sickness, so he assumes that things are status quo."

"You need to tell him, dopey," Jilly said.

"I'll tell him," Belle promised. "I will. Definitely. Any day now."

"AHEM," MARGARET SAID.

Kit's mind was in the garden of Truelove House, with Jilly, on a warm, clear moonlit night. His body was in the inn's business office, on a bright weekday morning, helping Margaret Greer with the computer system. He blinked and pulled himself back to the present.

"Uh, sorry," he mumbled. "My mind was wandering. Where were we?"

"You were explaining spreadsheets, more or less," Margaret said crisply. "Christopher, dear, Truelove House existed without spreadsheets for over fifty years, and it can exist without them now. Why don't you go see Jilly at the shop? I'm sure she'd be delighted to see you."

"Why don't *we* go see Jilly at the shop?" Kit said.

Margaret looked at him.

"If *I* drop in on Jilly, I'm going to look like a lovestruck fool," he said. "Which I am, but I'm clinging to the few pitifully small shreds of dignity I have left. If *we* drop in on Jilly, say on our way to the software store, I'll just look friendly and efficient."

Margaret snorted, shutting off her computer. "Jilly's shop is in the opposite direction from the software store, and Jilly's not stupid."

"Please?" Kit said. "I'll give you and your boyfriend from Chicago a great stock tip."

"Don't you think it's a little sad that a big strong guy like you needs to hide behind me? Not that there's not room."

"Yup. It's pathetic," Kit agreed.

"But I will go with you, just because I'm a sentimental sap. That stock tip better be good."

Twenty minutes later, Kit opened the door of Jilly's and gestured at Margaret to enter. Jilly was sitting at her desk, her face buried in cat.

"Jilly? Jilly, are you in there?"

"Yes. Unfortunately," Jilly said, raising a woeful face from Pankhurst's tufted back.

"What is it?" Margaret sat down next to her and took her hand. Kit stood behind her and patted her shoulder.

"My landlord. My lease is up in December, and he's going to double the rent."

"Why?" Margaret reached into the bag they'd brought and handed Jilly a doughnut. "Here. Sugar. Great for shock."

Kit sneezed. "Let me guess," he said. "Because he's a greedy bastard?"

"He is that." Jilly gave Pankhurst a final kiss, then gathered the cat in her arms. "You have to go out, kitty cat, otherwise the nice man here is going to get all sneezy," she said, depositing Pankhurst outdoors. "There's a new food court moving into that empty hotel on the corner," she added. "My landlord thinks that the value of this location has just gone up, and that he's thereby entitled to any extra profit I might make for the rest of my life."

"Will you get any extra business?" Kit asked.

"Not really. The people who come to a food court want chili dogs, not Coalport china."

"Could you find another space?" Kit pulled a chair closer to the desk, angled his large body onto its narrow rosewood seat and groped in the doughnut bag for a cinnamon bun.

"Here, have a napkin," Jilly said. "I can find something else if I absolutely have to, but it won't be the same. This place is just the right size, the location is great and my customers are used to it. Anyplace else...it just won't feel like home."

"What do the other shop owners say?" Margaret asked.

"You bought me a French cruller, my favorite," Jilly mourned, looking down at her doughnut, "and I'm too sad to eat it. This is so depressing. Here, you guys split it." She sighed. "Nice Mrs. Rosen, the lady who sells shells and stones, got the same letter I did. She was so upset I had to send her home." Jilly's eyes filled with tears. "Poor Mrs. Rosen. She's eighty-one, and it was Irving's shop. She'll never survive if she has to close it. It's all she has."

"What are you going to do about it?" Kit said, his mouth full of French cruller.

"Who's Irving?" Margaret asked.

"Irving is—was—Mrs. Rosen's husband. If Mrs. Rosen loses the shop, she'll lose her last real connection to him. As for my shop, I don't know what I'm going to do about it yet."

"Well, you definitely need to do something." Kit chose a third doughnut and took a healthy bite. "You can't just sit there. What about suing? A lawsuit ought to shake him up good."

"For God's sake, Kit, I just got the letter three minutes ago and already you're calling F. Lee Bailey."

"I don't think F. Lee Bailey does rent disputes, but I can put you in touch with my lawyer in Miami. He's terrific. You said you love this shop—aren't you gonna fight for it?"

"I don't have much fight in me at the moment."

Want to bet? Kit thought, looking at her gorgeously glum face. *I can make you mad in sixty seconds flat. And as a matter of fact, mad would be good for you. You let people take advantage of you too much. Claude. This landlord. Me, probably. Besides, I can't stand it when you're sad.*

"That's the problem with women," he pronounced loudly, folding his arms across his chest and propping his feet regally on the edge of a wicker planter. Margaret looked on, her eyebrows raised. "Basically, you're soft. If some goon tried to double a man's rent, he'd hit right back."

Jilly thumped his shins with her fist. "Feet off the furniture, you moron. Who raised you, Genghis and Mrs. Khan?" Jilly asked. "Right. A man would have bought a grenade launcher by now. And you think that's a good solution?"

"Not necessarily. But it's better than a bunch of dames crying." *Nah,* Kit decided, *she's not really mad until her chin sticks out.* "See," he said, "broads like you are all the same.

You look tough until the chips are down, but you cave in the minute anybody confronts you. You say you're feminists, but you just can't compete."

"Dames? Broads?" Jilly said through her teeth. She lifted her head and stuck her chin forward. "Please tell me I haven't actually slept with a man who calls women broads."

Bingo, Kit thought. *That got her going. Good.*

"Okay, so it's not the best word choice. But that's just semantics, babe," he said, his mouth twitching in amusement. "The point is, you're a bunch of wimps."

"Whereas you, you—Cro-Magnon creep, you and your big, hairy guy buddies are all perfect." Jilly stabbed at him with her finger. "You can't change a diaper or dry a plate and you have the emotional depth of a soap dish, but your goddamned way of doing things, which by the way has led to thousands of years of bloodshed and exterminated nine-tenths of the world's species, is better than a woman's."

"Right, basically," Kit said, sitting back in his chair.

He's just trying to help, Jilly told herself sternly.

No, he's not. He's just trying to get your goat.

And whatever a goat is, he's getting it.

"You know, Malone," she said. "This isn't just a male thing. This is a city thing. You big-city types are so paranoid you can barely breathe. This suing idea is typical. Someone's dog pees on your lawn and you ask for an indictment before it dries."

"A vulgar example, but exactly. Because unlike your island fruits and nuts, we live in the real world. You goofballs just stick your heads in the sand. Which, luckily, you've got a lot of."

"Great. You come to Key West—uninvited, I might

add—from a place where four-year-olds carry guns, and you have to insult my home?"

"That's my Jilly, always ready to defend her little island. I guess there's some fight left in you, after all." Kit grinned.

Jilly jumped out of her seat and reached over to give the neck of his T-shirt a yank. "Up," she said, pulling.

Startled, Kit half rose out of his chair. It was either that or get his shirt torn off. "What?"

"Up," she said, succeeding in getting him upright. "And out." She pushed at his shoulder until he was facing the door, braced both hands against his broad back and shoved. He tripped over a mahogany footstool, righting himself just in time to avoid crashing into a case full of crystal bottles. "If you break it, we mark it sold," Jilly said. "Out, now."

"Margaret—" Kit said.

"Margaret isn't going. You're going, and you're taking your creepy, citified, chauvinistic theories with you."

"I was just trying to get you to fight back," Kit said.

"You succeeded. I'm fighting back. I'm not in the mood, Malone. Donate your testosterone elsewhere. Somewhere in the world there's another perfectly nice woman just waiting for you to send her into an apoplectic rage. Don't waste all that talent on me. Share the wealth," Jilly said, hands on her hips, trying not to smile.

Kit loved her like this, exploding with guts and smarts and fire, even when he was the target of it. "Remember," he said, "we're having dinner with the guys. Can you get to Ernest's by seven?"

"I have no intention of having dinner with any guys, tonight or ever. But don't worry. When I don't show up, you can always sue me." Jilly opened the door and pushed him through.

"Jillian?" Kit said from the sidewalk.

"What?" Jilly paused with her hand on the door. "Oh, I know. I have silver polish or stencil paint or something equally dumb on my nose."

"No," Kit said softly. "I love you, babe." He grinned at her and was gone.

10

EACH YEAR, THE KEY WEST Volleyball League hosted a huge, festive, boisterous Labor Day party. It was a casual and rowdy occasion geared toward casual and rowdy guests. Children ate too much and ran around in circles, adults ate too much and snuck off behind the trees to neck, and everyone got too much late afternoon sun. Almost all of the guests were members or friends of one of the league's six feuding teams, rivals for the annual trophy. It was a dull year which didn't have at least one screaming argument about volleyball or one broken nose.

Jilly didn't ordinarily think of herself as the party type, but she was looking forward to this year's bash. She always enjoyed sitting around with her Conch Team pals talking, reminiscing and trashing their arch rivals, the Lobster Team. This year, having Kit to go with added to the pleasure. Assuming, of course, that she could ever figure out what to wear.

She stood in her bedroom, pulled off her lemon yellow shorts and dropped them on the floor. Ninety percent of the clothes she owned were already in the same pile. She wanted to look sexy, but she didn't want it to seem like she was trying. She wanted to be casual, but she didn't want to look like a cute little girl.

"That's a decent pile of dirty clothes on your floor there," Kit said from behind her. "With a little practice, kid, you could be great."

"They're not dirty clothes, they're clean ones. I can't figure out what to wear to the party." Jilly held a denim coverall against her chest and squinted at herself in the mirror. "This makes me look like Rosie the Riveter. Why didn't I notice that before?" she said.

Kit watched appreciatively as she dropped the coverall, leaving herself clad only in a starched white shirt. "What you have on now works for me."

"I know," Jilly said. "It'll work for every other guy at the party, too."

"Right. Bad idea. Forget I spoke." Kit pulled off his mud-smudged T-shirt, rolled it up into a ball and tossed it into the corner of the room. "It's company for your stuff," he said defensively, catching her admonitory glance.

Jilly tilted her head pensively for a moment, then pounced. "That shirt," she said, tugging at the hem of the clean short-sleeved black cotton shirt he was starting to pull over his head. "I need it."

"This is what you want to wear?" Kit's head appeared through the neck hole. He looked at her skeptically. "I know you like things baggy, but this is going to look like a nightgown on you. Morticia Addams's nightgown."

"Look." Jilly took off the white shirt. She tugged the shirt back up over his shoulders and pulled it over her own head. She fished a sheer black chiffon skirt out of the pile and shook out its thousands of tiny pleats, then tied the long bottom of the tee in a knot over one hip so that it stretched snugly around her rear. Rummaging under her bed she found a pair of strappy low-heeled black sandals and slid her bare feet into them. "How about this?" She pivoted, sending the transparent skirt billowing gracefully around her bare tanned legs.

"Someday you're going to have to explain to me how you manage it," Kit said.

"What?"

"This thing you do with clothes. Obvious female clothes ploys I can defend myself against, but I'm lost with you." Kit sighed, choosing another T-shirt from the dresser drawer. "Seriously, that outfit looks great. Do you think the leash I'm going to have to put around your neck will ruin it?"

"Are you calling me a dog, Malone?" Jilly teased, heading toward the bathroom to put on some makeup.

Kit dropped onto the bed to lace his sneakers. "Never, Sanderson. I'm just feeling a bit possessive. There's gonna be a lot of horny guys at this party, you know. I just don't want any of them getting any ideas."

"Oh, that's okay. I can't go to the party, anyway," Jilly said, putting her lipstick away. "I have to stay home and clean up all these clothes."

THE PARTY WAS IN FULL swing by the time they arrived at six. The league had rented out the state park complex on the beachy, unspoiled key of Bahia Honda. Strings of pink and yellow Japanese paper lanterns lit up the clubhouse, lawn and shoreline. A bluegrass band played while couples spun and dipped. There were lines at the beer kegs, longer lines at the grills where ribs and burgers and blackened catfish flamed, and down on the beach, clam pits and blankets and impromptu volleyball games. As Kit parked the Jaguar, the sun was just beginning to set in pink-and-gold splendor.

Kit draped his arm around Jilly's shoulders and strolled with her to get a drink. Every three feet or so someone stopped them to greet Jilly. People talked to her like she was their best friend, Kit thought, and Jilly returned their affection, giving hugs and asking about their children, their businesses or their lives. He drew her more closely within the shelter of his arm. She leaned against him happily, trusting and secure.

"You really do fit in here, don't you?" he said pensively, once they were alone again.

"Yes, I do. It's the first place I've ever really felt at home." Jilly smiled up at him. "You fit in here, too, more than you think."

"I know." Kit paused. *Tell her you need to go to Miami this Thursday,* an inner voice prodded him. *Ask her to go with you.*

She's already given you the answer, he thought in response. *This is her home. She would have offered to come to Miami before, if that's what she wanted.*

Tell her anyway. It's too late already. Tell her now.

"Jilly," he began, "there's something—"

"Jilly!" three enthusiastic voices chorused from behind them. "Killer! We thought you guys were never gonna come."

"Shep, Curly and Moe. Perfect timing," Kit said, closing his eyes. Jilly darted him a quick curious glance, but he shook his head and let the guys lead them off to a table. He'd waited this long, he thought helplessly, what was another hour or so? *Too long,* a voice in his brain told him.

JILLY BUMPED INTO JEFF on the way back from the ladies' room. "Hey, beautiful. Great skirt," he said. "Sexy."

"Thanks. Where is everyone?"

"Playin' ball, down on the beach." Jeff wiggled his right arm. "My wrist hurts, so I decided to sit it out. Wanna wander over to the pier with me, since my gal, Molly, and your guy, Malone, are both swatting a ball around?"

"Sure." They walked companionably onto the pier, a rickety wooden structure jutting into the waves. Jeff leaned his elbows on the railing and sighed with contentment. "This is great. Look at that moon. So, babe, ya going with Malone to Miami?" he asked.

"Miami? When?"

"Thursday." Jeff always looked a little confused—Jilly figured it was just something about his bone structure— but now he looked a lot confused. "You know, when he goes back to work. Thursday. I was almost sure. Did I get the day wrong?"

"No. No, I just wasn't thinking," Jilly said quickly, thinking. Thursday? Miami? Either Jeff was out of his mind or drunk or both, which was possible, or there was something Kit had chosen not to tell her. A very big something. "I guess I'm just having trouble focusing on it," she improvised, not wanting Jeff to see how confused *she* was.

"Yeah, I know what you mean. He's, like, part of things here, ya know? Pretty amazing, when you think about it. But hey, let's not get too morbid. We'll be seeing him a lot."

Jilly kept her voice casual. "I guess so."

"Come on, babe. I mean, you're sure gonna see him. That's the thing about being married, you have to see the person, whether you want to or not." Jeff guffawed. "That's exactly why Moll and I aren't married."

"Married?" Jilly tried to fight the sense that she'd been dropped into a parallel universe. A strange, hideously embarrassing universe in which 90 percent of the men on the planet knew things about her life that she didn't know herself. "Me?"

"Yeah, you. Who else? You and Killer. Jeez. You're kinda slow on the uptake tonight, kid."

"Oh." Jilly cast about for an answer. "Well. Married," she repeated brightly. "Whenever that will be."

"Me, I'm surprised the two of you haven't set a date. Malone sure was hot to trot the night he told us about it.

Might as well get it over with. Like, the sooner y'all get married, the sooner Malone's money becomes community property, right?"

"Right," Jilly said gamely.

Jeff gave her a gentle punch in the arm. "Seriously, hon, he's great. You're great. You're going to have great kids. I mean, Malone wasn't sure about the kids part, but I figure if he was already thinking about it a couple of weeks after he met you, it's gotta be in the bag."

"Sure. Babies. Terrific," Jilly muttered. "And just how many did he decide we'd have?"

"Huh?" Jeff looked at her.

Jilly put her arm around his brawny shoulders and squeezed. "Never mind," she said. "I'm just a little surprised he talked so much about it."

"Well, that's Malone. He's a direct kind of guy. At least, he sure as hell ain't shy."

Sure, Jilly thought, her mind whirling. *Christopher Malone. Mr. Fearless. Mr. Frank and Open. Who hasn't said one word about going to Miami, bringing me to Miami, finding a way to make our lives fit together, marrying me, having kids or anything else. Which means one of two things. Either he doesn't really want me, despite the lip service to our relationship he's given to his buddies. Or he's playing some kind of weird controlling manipulative game with me. Maybe he thinks that the longer he waits, the more grateful I'll be. Maybe he thinks I'm so smitten, it's just a forgone conclusion.*

None of this sounds like Kit, some reasonable part of her brain objected.

Kit is going back to Miami on Thursday and you didn't know it. Kit is blabbing to half the men in Key West about you and your future, right down to the kids you will or will not have, and you didn't know it.

Face it, you fool. You can't know what sounds like Kit Malone, because you don't know Kit Malone at all.

The worst thing, she discovered, was that she didn't know what to feel. Part of her was furious. Part her of was confused. Part of her was numb. She had to figure out what to do, but she didn't know whether to kill Kit, kill herself or just run away and hide.

She thought for a moment, then spoke. "You're right. Kit's not shy. When did you guys discuss this stuff, anyway?"

"A couple of weeks ago, somewhere. We all kinda overdid the alcohol thing, so it's a little blurry. It was a riot, though. I remember that Malone was really funny, going on about marriage and kids, and you being shy, and Claude, and all."

Jilly clenched her fists and gritted her jaw. *Good*, she thought. *Now I know how to feel.* Kit had talked about Miami and their marriage and their hypothetical kids three weeks ago? Three weeks ago he'd spilled his guts to his buddies—*her* buddies—and since then there hadn't been a single quiet moment when he could have said something to her? And not only had he discussed the most private details of her life without her permission, he'd had the gall to *laugh* about it?

Jilly felt a wave of calm wash over her. First, she thought, she had to get out of this conversation with Jeff without hurting his feelings. It wasn't his fault. He was bumbling and naive, maybe, but he had only the best intentions. Naturally he'd assume that anything Kit told the guys, Kit had also told her. Anybody would assume that, except Kit Malone.

Jeff and Jilly stood for a moment, leaning against the railing, looking at the moon. *Thank God for friends*, Jilly thought. She was grateful for Jeff's solid, dopey, predictable presence, even if he had unwittingly killed her relationship with his great pal Kit Malone. "You're a good guy, you moron," she said.

"You, too, babe. Don't be sad," Jeff said, petting her arm. "You'll see him a lot. He's only going to spend some time in Miami. It's not the moon."

Jilly kissed his cheek. *As far as I'm concerned,* she thought, *it might as well be.* "Listen, I'd better go. See you at the game Thursday, okay?"

"Yeah," Jeff answered. "Shrimp Team. Bunch of losers. We'll kill 'em."

It's not them I'm worried about killing, Jilly thought. "I'm looking forward to it," she lied.

Now, she thought, *I just have to figure out how to get out of here before I scream or throw up.* She could feel herself begin to shake a little with confusion and distress. She didn't want anyone to see that, and she didn't want to see Kit, because if she saw him she'd have to punch him in the nose in front of all her friends. Maybe she could hitch a ride home from someone, or at least call a taxi. Luckily darkness had fallen while she'd been on the pier with Jeff. She took off her sandals and started walking, making a wide circle around the clusters of people at the clam pits and volleyball nets, trying not to catch the eye of anyone she knew.

As she crossed the sand she caught sight of Kit at one of the big bonfires, a blond woman at his side. Kit laughed and the woman laughed, then the woman reached in the pocket of her skintight jeans and pulled out a card, and Kit stuck the card in his own pocket, looking down at her. The woman tossed her mane of strawberry blond hair and they both laughed again. Already upset, Jilly felt her face flush in humiliation. *Around twenty-three, and great you-know-whats,* she thought, mortified. *Brandy, I presume?*

This guy's definitely playing a game, she concluded. *But it ain't volleyball.*

"Jilly," Kit called. "Jilly, wait up." She started to run, but his long legs covered distance faster than hers and within moments he caught up to where she strode breathlessly along what seemed like a mile of sand. "What are you doing, Sanderson? I've been looking for you."

"Why?" Jilly said, keeping her back to him.

"Why? What do you mean, why?" Kit put his hand on her shoulder and Jilly shrugged it off.

"Get your hands off me," she said.

"Jilly, what the hell is wrong?"

"I don't know, Kit. Why don't you tell me?"

"Meaning what?" Jilly could almost feel his body tense behind her.

"Meaning nothing. Forget it. I'm not going to talk about this now."

"Oh, yes, you are." Suddenly Kit's voice was grim.

Jilly whirled to face him. "Really? Who says? Who died and left you king?"

Looming over her in the warm torchlight of the beach, Kit looked big and dangerous. "I'm not a king. I am your lover, and I deserve to know what's bothering you," he said.

"I have an idea," Jilly told him. "I'll tell all my girl-friends, and maybe if you're lucky one of them will pass it on to you."

"Could you be a little clearer, please?"

"Let's see. How about, half the people in Key West know about your schedule for returning to Miami, your plans for me, my history with Claude, our impending marriage and, let's see, your ambivalence about children. All things about which I know nothing. Is that clear enough?"

"Yes." *Damn*, he thought. *This is your fault, Malone. Fix it.*

He tried to lighten her mood so that he'd have a chance to explain. "Not half the people, actually. Only half the guys."

"Really?" Jilly glared at him. "Well, I'm glad you didn't tell little blond Brandy, there, over by the fire. It's certainly good to know that someone knows less about my life than I do."

"Her name is Cheryl Willis. She's a computer consultant. I thought she might be able to help Margaret with the inn's system."

"Sure. Except that you were supposed to be playing volleyball."

"I asked Ned to take my place. I came to look for you. Come on, Jilly," Kit said, trying to be patient.

"Well, I can see how you would confuse the two of us. All I need is a breast job, a dye job and a lobotomy, and we'd be identical twins."

"Jilly, this is getting us nowhere."

"There's nowhere to get. Look," Jilly said, frustrated. She started to walk up the beach again. Doggedly Kit tagged behind her. "I'm sorry I brought little Miss Microchip up. As far as I'm concerned you're free to screw every busty blonde from here to Niagara Falls. Your sex drive isn't the point. Your big mouth is. I resent hearing that every intimate detail of my life has been discussed with my friends behind my back, is the point."

"Fine. Let's start there. Who told you about this?"

Jilly reached the dunes and kept walking, threading her way along the path through the beach grass, aiming for the clubhouse. The sounds of the party drifted toward her on the cooling breeze. For one disoriented moment she was consumed by the desire to slip into Kit's warm arms. Then she remembered. She lifted her chin and looked at him, wary. "Jeff told me," she said.

"Oh," Kit answered sarcastically. *"Jeff."*

"Right. Jeff."

"Right. *Jeff."* Kit nodded.

"This is ridiculous," Jilly said. "And don't you use that tone of voice. Jeff happens to be one of my best friends."

"He's a friend of mine, too," Kit snapped, starting to get annoyed. "That's why I know that he's an idiot. I know that he has a heart of gold and the perceptiveness of a dead trout. I know that about 90 percent of the subtleties of a conversation sail directly over his basically thick head. I know that. Why don't you know that, Jilly?"

"I know it. I don't care about it, Kit. It doesn't matter whether it was Jeff or Ned or the Easter Bunny. I don't like hearing about your plans for me and Miami and marriage and children from someone else. I don't like finding out that my feelings and insecurities were discussed in public. I don't like knowing that my past or my relationship with you were trivialized enough to become the subject of riotous laughter among a bunch of drunks in a bar. I don't like you announcing plans you haven't even talked to me about. I just don't like it, damn you."

"Well, you know what?" Kit said, steaming now. His eyes glittered with anger. Even in the dim light Jilly could see the lines bracketing his mouth and forehead, the furious set of his jaw. "I don't like it either, lady. I don't like having some tipsy guy's version of events being taken as the only possible truth. I don't like letting a woman into my life who can't even bother to listen to my side of things. And I sure as hell don't like being condemned as the villain before I'm even given a chance to explain."

"Fine." Jilly clasped her arms across her chest. "What is the truth?"

"I'm happy to tell you. The car is this way."

"I'm not going in the car."

"Yes, you are. We need to finish this and you need to get home to Key West, which is miles away. What you do when you get there is your business."

"Fine." It wasn't fine, not really, but having to ride home with some jolly party guest would be even worse than riding home with Kit. At least the car was private. She followed him toward the parking lot, barely able to keep up with his furious strides.

Despite the warmth of the night, the Jaguar felt chilly. Jilly buckled her seat belt and rubbed her arms. With grim efficiency Kit pulled away from the parking lot. Being in the car with him was horrible, Jilly realized. It was too hard, being this close to his body, close enough to feel his warmth and smell his cologne, when their minds were so far apart.

"Whether or not I mishandled this, and I probably did, you're wrong," Kit said once they were on the highway. Jilly seemed to shake beside him. She was obviously tired and chilled. She broke his heart. He groped in the back for his jean jacket and dropped it on her lap, but kept his voice flat. *She started this*, he thought. She had decided to attack him, rather than giving him a chance. He was willing to explain, but he was damned if he was going to roll over for her. "I didn't cheapen you or betray you or announce any bloody plans. I didn't know how to approach you—you were sending out completely mixed signals, and I didn't want to mess it up," he continued. "I asked for help from the guys, because they know you and love you. They asked me what my intentions were, and I told them I was serious about you. Then I came home and told you I was serious about you, and the truth is that I've always acted like I was serious about you. Not for one minute have I ever given you any reason to doubt that."

"Except that I'm the last person to know that you're leaving me on Thursday."

"I am not leaving you, Jilly. For God's sake. I was going to go to work on Thursday and Friday and come back Friday night and spend the weekend with you trying to figure out some way of dealing with our lives. I'm sorry you heard about the trip that way. But I happen to have a life, a job and a partner who has every right to want me to get on with doing that job. I don't see why I should have to feel so guilty about fulfilling my obligations, just because my obligations happen to be located in a town you hate."

"You shouldn't," Jilly said. Jerkily she pulled Kit's jacket more closely around her shoulders. She was freezing, she thought, from the inside out. "Look, Kit, I just don't know where this thing between us is going. Maybe there's just no place for it to go at all. You're committed to the city, to your job, to your life. I'm committed to Key West. We didn't fit together at the beginning, and the truth is we don't fit together now. Why don't we just keep it simple and let it go?"

"Oh, that's real simple," Kit repeated bitterly, pulling the car off the highway and into the heart of Key West. "Thanks so much. That's your idea of love? I screw up once and I'm fired?"

"No. But what's *your* idea of love? That it's making every decision, calling every shot? Coming back down to Key West without calling me, hiding your feelings from me while you check me out with our friends, telling me how I need to fight for my business, protecting me from your plans until you think I need to hear them? Do you think love means that you know me or my life or my needs better than I do? Because that's what I had with Claude, Kit. Without the passion, without the laughs, but the same basic deal. Claude led and I followed, and it practically killed me. And I can't go through it again, not for you, not for anyone."

"You know, Jilly, you're right. I do expect to control things. I do shade the truth to protect you. And it's wrong. But you know what else? I can learn to change, and I *have* changed."

"Kit—"

"No. Let me finish. Because of you, I've learned what it means to want a woman more than I want anything else in the world. I've learned what it means to share my life with a woman, not just carefully selected parts of me, the whole damned thing. I'm not perfect. I screw up sometimes, but I'm learning. What have you learned, Jilly?"

Kit braked with a screech, jerking the car into Park. They were in front of her own house, Jilly realized. She'd had no idea they were home. He opened his door, strode around to her side and opened hers as well. They stood faced off against each other in the moonlight—only inches away, Jilly realized, from the place they'd kissed for the first time.

Kit didn't seem to notice. His voice was low and cold. His eyes were glacial. "What have you learned about sharing with me?" he asked roughly. "When have you tried to be part of my life? Did you ever show any real interest in my apartment, or my office, or my city? Hell, no. You want me, sure, but you want me on your terms, and you just ignore any part of me that doesn't fit into your world. Well, that's too bad. My life was empty and incomplete before I met you. But it's a part of who I am. I'm not going to throw it all away. And a woman who really loves me wouldn't expect me to."

"I do love you, and I do want to share your life," Jilly said. "I'm hesitant, and I'm scared, and I can't risk another mistake like Claude. Why can't you understand that?"

"I do understand, Jilly." Kit stared into her eyes. She

was trembling and upset. Her eyes were wild and her cap of hair was mussed and she looked fragile with his big denim jacket wrapped around her small frame. Hardening his heart, he went on. "I understand that it always comes back to this same place, it always comes back to your past. Again and again I've tried to prove myself. Again and again I've tried to arrange my entire life so it won't hurt or scare you. That's why I didn't mention Miami or marriage to you. But you were right. That doesn't work. I'll own up to my own mistakes with you, gladly, but I can't keep paying for what Claude or your parents did. I can't undo the pain they caused you. If we're going to make it, you have to trust me enough to give me a clean slate. You have to move on, let the past go. And it's time we both faced it, Jilly." Kit paused a moment before he spoke, his voice rough and low and heartbreakingly final. "That's something you're just not willing to do." Giving her one long, burning look, he got back in the Jaguar, pulled the door shut behind him, and drove away. Helpless, Jilly watched the taillights disappear.

JILLY SAT AT THE DESK in her shop, polishing the silver she'd left unfinished since the morning she met Kit Malone.

Two days had passed since Kit had driven away from her house. His room at the inn was empty and neat. His toothbrush and a few extra clothes were still in Jilly's bedroom. She had started to box them up the previous night, but the mere act of touching his holey Yale sweatshirt made her cry. She told herself it was ludicrous and undignified to cry over anything marked Yale, and decided to leave his stuff alone.

And then she'd sat up half the night, thinking. The problem was that everything else reminded her of him, too. The silver polish, for example. Jilly felt her eyes fill up and reached into her desk drawer to get a tissue. The tissue reminded her of Kit, too, sneezing away that first day in her shop.

She blew her nose, hard, and put two fingers in her mouth, whistling.

"Come here, Pankhurst," she said when the cat's tortoiseshell head emerged from under a settee. Pankhurst jumped onto the desk and Jilly rubbed her face against Pankhurst's tawny, tufty coat. "Look," she murmured, "it wouldn't be so bad. I could be a spinster with a shop and a cat and have a perfectly productive life."

Pankhurst looked at her with glowing green eyes. "Don't look so skeptical," Jilly said, then sighed. "All right, look skeptical. It would be pretty bad. It would be dreadful."

"Are you talking to that ridiculous feline again? Haven't we done this before?" Margaret's voice called from the door. Pankhurst leapt off Jilly's lap, startled.

"Don't remind me," Jilly said. "Where are the doughnuts?"

"No doughnuts," Margaret told her, sitting down. "When you called, you said this was a business meeting, so I thought doughnuts would set the wrong tone."

"Doughnuts never set the wrong tone. Now, as for the business—" Jilly wiped her hands on the polish cloth and flipped through the folders on her desk "—I would like you to consider the possibility of turning Lavinia's empty apartment into space for two small shops, an antique shop and a shell, gem and mineral shop. The apartment is on the first floor and has its own utilities and entrance—it even has a window we could use for display. The shops would draw tourists and maybe future guests to the inn, and the inn would provide potential customers for the shops. The retailers, myself and Mrs. Rosen, would pay rent, of course. I've suggested a figure and given you estimates of the various costs and revenues. I'll also bring this up with my co-owner, of course, but I think it would make sense for everyone involved."

"Well, child, I, for one, think it's a great idea," Margaret said. "I'll look at the numbers, but it sounds fine. Very clever, in fact."

Jilly handed over the folder of estimates. "We broads may not be aggressive, but we're smart."

"You'll be losing square footage, though. Will you have enough room for all of the stuff you have here?"

"No." Jilly smiled, a little tremulously. "I won't need it. I have other plans."

"Give me a hint."

"I'll tell you as soon as I know for sure. Nothing's set yet, and until it is, I have to be discreet."

"Oh, are you being discreet?" Margaret said. "I thought you were just being irritating."

Jilly laughed. "I am, probably. But I can't help it."

"You know, I expected you to be heartbroken and pining. Instead, you're bubbling with ideas and schemes, mysterious as they may be. Does your good mood mean you've talked to Kit?"

"No, it doesn't, and no, I haven't. But I'm keeping his advice in mind."

"What advice?"

"He said I should let the past go. That I should learn to fight back for what I want. Well, I'm fighting."

"Good." Margaret regarded her friend with affection. "Lavinia would be proud of you, and I am, too."

"Thanks. Wish me luck," Jilly said, touching Margaret's warm, capable hand.

"I seem to recall that your cat handles the wish department, but I'll be thinking of you." Margaret stood and picked up the proposal folder. "And by the way, you have silver polish on your nose."

JILLY SPENT THE REST OF the day making calls to Miami real-estate agents, lining up appointments for the next day. Then she gave Pankhurst a kiss, locked the shop door behind her and went home.

The next morning she woke up nervous but resolved. She slipped into her favorite summer outfit, a cinnamon-colored washed silk shell paired with a long silk sarong patterned in cinnamon, gold and black. She put on earrings and eyeliner and a hefty shot of perfume. She tossed her handbag into the back of her car, which she'd barely used that summer, and started the long drive to Miami. She made it to the South Beach district in good time. The sun sparkled on the rows of art-deco buildings with their frivolous pastel trims.

You know, she thought sheepishly, *Miami doesn't look half-bad*.

"This is it," she said to the Realtor a few hours later, standing in the middle of an empty storefront. "There's someone I need to show it to, but you can assume I'll take it. I'll stop by later, arrange for the deposit and sign the lease."

She walked to a pay phone and called Kit's office. After a brief wrangle, a secretary finally agreed to put Mr. Malone on the line.

"Malone here," he said.

"Kit. It's Jilly. I'm genuinely sorry to bother you, but could you spare me fifteen minutes or so?"

There was a pause. Jilly could almost hear him thinking. "Now?" he said.

"Yes. I'm in Miami. At Palmetto and Fourth, in South

Beach. Not far." She waited, but he remained silent. "It's sort of...an emergency."

"All right," he said, his voice still gruff and wary. She gave him the address and walked back into the empty store.

A few minutes later, Kit pushed open the grimy front door. "Jilly?" His voice echoed in the bleak dusty room. He looked around, frowning, trying to figure out what he was doing in this apparently abandoned place.

"Here," she said, emerging from the back alley. "Thank you for coming."

"What's the emergency? Are you all right?"

"No, I'm not. I'm lonely, Kit," she said.

Kit's face was impassive, uncompromising in the shadowy light. "This is a lonely place," he said, his voice neutral.

"No, it's not. It's just empty, and everything's empty when you're starting something new." Jilly took a deep breath. "And it's not where I'm lonely."

Kit raised one eyebrow.

"I'm lonely in my life, Kit. I don't like my life without you in it anymore." Jilly stepped closer, resting her hands lightly against the middle of his chest. "But you were right," she continued softly. "You can't make yourself over for me. You can't abandon your life. We can't live in the past, anyone's past. It was unfair of me to expect you to."

"I'm glad you understand, Jilly. But as you pointed out, our lives still don't fit. Where does this leave us?" Kit heard the harshness in his tone, but he couldn't soften it. If he softened his voice, if he held the soft feminine hands touching him so trustingly, if he looked into her eyes, he would drown, or cry, or beg, or just take the decision away from her. He wanted her more than he had ever wanted

anyone. The past few days without her had been agony.
But it was her decision, and if they were to have any
chance at all she had to make it willingly. He steeled himself and stayed silent.

"It leaves us here." Jilly waved at the dusty echoing
space around her. "I'm going to move my Key West shop
into the empty space in Truelove House, with your permission as co-owner, of course. That's a smaller, cheaper
space than I have now, and I'd like to use the savings to
open a new shop here, in Miami."

"Here?"

"Yes. I like this location, although I haven't signed the
lease yet. Once the new shop is open, I thought I would begin by spending half my time in each place. Mrs. Rosen
will watch the Key West shop when I'm not there, and I'll
find someone to work in this one part-time."

Jilly stopped, watching Kit's face. He made no move to
touch her, but he hadn't yet pushed her away. *Don't
chicken out now, Jilly, you wimpy, fluffy, crybaby dame,* she
told herself, and smiled. "Even if I have to make some adjustments, for decorating projects and so on, that will give
me half the week in Miami. And...I'd like to spend every
minute of my spare time here with you."

Kit looked down at her, his face grave. "Are you saying
that you're willing to make some adjustments to fit my
schedule?" he asked.

"Yes," Jilly said warily. *Well, at least he isn't saying no.
Yet.*

"For example, I'll be driving to Key West early each
Thursday evening for an important athletic commitment,
then staying in the Keys until Sunday night. You would
need to work around that. It's not negotiable."

"I can handle that." Jilly ran one finger under the edge
of Kit's maroon silk tie.

"Please, Ms. Sanderson." Kit couldn't stop his voice from warming a little, making him sound much more like the helplessly lovesick, pathetically relieved fool he was. "This is a business discussion and we have a great deal to cover. I'm a busy man, after all. Next item. I have an interior design job for you, and it can't wait. A penthouse in a high-rise building. The owner is experiencing an imminent...change of life-style. Perhaps you could come examine the space and then we'll discuss your input."

"That won't be necessary. I can give you my input in a single word."

"And that would be...?"

"Inappropriate," Jilly said.

"Ah." Kit nodded wisely. "That sounds excellent. Inappropriate is always good. But not illegal. I'm afraid I'm unable to be a party to any such arrangement not recognized under relevant law." Finally he smiled down at her, a smile he'd only recently learned he had, a big, silly, utterly sincere, totally uncorporate smile.

"Give me a break, goofball," Jilly said, smiling back. "I'm willing to eat crow, but you're going to have to do better than that."

"I love you, Jilly. I can't live without you, even if I wanted to—which I never really did. If you would agree to marry me, you would make me a very happy man. Please, Jilly?" Kit leaned down and kissed her lips. She slipped her arms around him and kissed him back.

"Yes, Kit," she said when he released her. "Double yes. Yes squared. Yes to the max. Yes on toast. When?"

"Soon. Whenever you want. It's up to you. I'm through making all the decisions around here."

"Uh-huh. Sure." Jilly rolled her eyes. "Come on, I'll walk you back to your office. I think I've already pushed Hank far enough."

Kit handed Jilly her handbag and walked with her toward the door. "This is a great store. What are you going to call it? Jilly's North? Jilly's 2? Son—oops—daughter of Jilly's?"

"I thought I'd call it Mabel's," Jilly said.

"Good idea. That would be a kind of cute name for our daughter, too." Kit closed the door of the empty shop behind them and took Jilly's hand, guiding her down the street toward his office.

"Daughter?" Jilly nudged Kit in the ribs with her elbow. "Ah, yes, the famous children we may or may not be having, depending on whom you ask." Kit made a face at her. "Please," she said, "let's not rush." She tilted her head to one side. "Nah. Mabel's just too weird—all the kids would tease her. How about Brandy?"

"Funny." Kit grinned. "You know, we better hurry up and get a cat. Every shop needs a cat."

"Yeah. I need to think up another good feminist name."

"Oh, no." Vehemently Kit shook his head. "No way."

"What do you mean, no way?" Jilly paused to let a bicyclist pass, then started across the street.

"No way," Kit said, catching up with her. "One feminist cat is enough."

"Forget it, bozo. It's gonna be my shop and it's gonna be my cat. Susan, for Susan B. Anthony? Woolf, for Virginia Woolf? Or something more modern? Greer? Friedan? Steinem?"

"Steinem? *Steinem?* Give me a break, Sanderson, that's ridiculous, even for you. Miami is my turf, and I'm picking the name. I'm gonna think of a good guy name. Bruiser, or Spike, or Buster, maybe. Or something historical. Bluebeard? Don Juan? Henry VIII? Or maybe you can just call it Sir. It'll be good practice for our marriage."

Jilly stood in the middle of the busy Miami sidewalk and

laughed out loud, giddy with the pleasure of being with Kit again, thrilled by the thought of being with Kit forever. "Sir? *Sir?* In your dreams, Malone."

Kit stopped short. A navy-suited woman with a cellular phone bumped into him hard. "Idiot," she said, moving on. "Watch what you're doing." Kit ignored her, and the people around her, and the stoplights and the skyscrapers and the cars. He picked Jilly up and held her in his arms and whirled her around in a big, breathless, dizzying circle. Jilly dropped her handbag. Her left shoe flew off and landed in the gutter. Laughing, she kicked off the other shoe and wiggled her bare feet in the air.

Kit held her, grinning and triumphant. For a moment Jilly could have sworn that she glimpsed the sheen of moisture in his beautiful gray eyes. Or maybe it was just the tears welling up in her own.

"Yeah. In my dreams, Sanderson," he said huskily, kissing her. "In my dreams, Sanderson, that's exactly where we are."

Epilogue

TRUELOVE HOUSE HAD NEVER looked better, everyone in Key West agreed. And neither had its owners.

What better day on which to get married, Jilly and Kit had decided, than on Lavinia and Sam's anniversary, the reopening date of the newly refurbished Truelove House bed-and-breakfast inn?

Beginning at twilight on November 12, guests began to arrive at the inn's glossy front door. Inside, fresh rose, periwinkle and aqua paint gleamed on the walls. The old brass chandeliers and hot-water faucets, doorknobs and drawer pulls were mirror bright. Snowy new lace curtains peeped from between shuttered windows. Soft hooked rugs, shaded lamps, antique prints and scattered throw pillows gave each room its own distinct character, while the floral chintzes of cushions and draperies gave the inn a harmonious traditional air.

Bottles of chilled champagne rested in silver buckets. Every vase in the hotel cascaded with flowers. In the center of the arrangement on the bridal table rested a single tightly budded pink rose, stolen for the occasion by Kit Malone from the neighbor two doors down.

In honor of his life as a slick Miami money manager, Kit Malone wore impeccable black tie. In honor of his new half-time existence as a Key West beach bum, he wore a silk cummerbund printed with palm trees and tropical fish. In honor of his membership on the Conch Team, he

had an aching bruise at the angle of his left jaw, acquired
when he was hit on the side of the head with a volleyball
serve while distracted by a fantasy about his wife-to-be's
breasts. A small gold earring glinted in his left ear.

In honor of the bridal tradition, Jilly Sanderson wore
lace with tiny seed pearls. In acknowledgment of the fact
that this was, after all, her second marriage, the dress was
not white but the palest shade of shell pink. In honor of
Kit's often expressed admiration for her slender figure and
beautiful legs, it was a form-fitting sheath with long
sleeves, a low square neck and a wicked slit up the side,
which disclosed the sheerest of blush-colored stockings
and dyed-to-match shoes ornamented with the tiniest of
pink silk bows. Hidden by the dress's lace sleeves, a ban-
dage wrapped the wrist she had sprained when she served
the ball that hit her fantasizing husband-to-be in the jaw.
Her opal-and-diamond earrings matched her small opal-
and-diamond wedding ring, a Malone family heirloom.

Neither Jilly nor Kit had really planned on a big wedding, but somehow it had seemed poor spirited not to let
all the friends who had helped their romance along play a
role. Benjamin Knowles, delighted by the happy resolu-
tion of Lavinia's unorthodox will, officiated at the brief
service. Hank Weinstein and the three Conch Team men
acted as ushers, balanced by Belle Lincoln, now in her fifth
month of pregnancy, Margaret Greer and Maisie Du-
Maurier, of whom Jilly had become quite fond in the
course of Maisie's endless house decoration project. Olivia
and Katherine Lincoln acted as flower girls. Mrs. Rosen
stood in for the mother of the bride and a twinkling Angus
MacPherson gave the bride away. Matthew and Nathaniel
Lincoln played no official role but were sighted in and
around the groom's Jaguar carrying old shoes, empty cans
and rice.

The big portrait of Lavinia and Sam Malone smiled down approvingly from over the mantel.

Two hundred guests watched, clapped, cried, laughed, ate, drank and generally filled the inn to bursting. Mattie, the plant lady, came, as did Margaret's friend Al from Chicago, both of them considerably enriched by the Allied stock Kit had recommended for them. The Sanderson family of Atlanta and F. Claude Henderson, Jr. were not invited. Brandy Cole was invited but did not attend. Pankhurst and the couple's new cat, Iron John, feasted on scraps of the wedding dinner in the kitchen.

At nine-thirty, Kit caught Jilly's eye, raised one rakish black eyebrow and tilted his head toward the garden.

Outside, the Key West air was moist and balmy. A cool breeze rustled among the fragrant leaves. Kit had deliberately left the garden just a little overgrown, so that it still seemed private and romantic.

He led his bride to a secluded bench and settled her on his lap. Over their heads, a mimosa shed its sweet scent and a warbler sang. Somewhere over the tops of the garden's trees a round yellow moon hung low in the sky.

"Hello, husband," Jilly said.

"Hello, wife," Kit answered. "Somehow I feel as though I haven't seen you in years."

"Weddings do seem to take on a life of their own. But it was a lovely ceremony, wasn't it?" Jilly kicked off her pretty but uncomfortable pumps and leaned back against Kit's chest. "I can't decide whether my favorite part was when Ben lost the words to the wedding service or when Olivia decided to eat the rose petals for breakfast."

"Hey," Kit said. "What about the part where I said I'd love and cherish you until I died?"

"Oh, that." Jilly smiled into his gorgeous gray eyes. "The only problem with that part was that I was convinced

I was going to cry or faint or both. I was trembling so hard
I wasn't sure I could keep standing up."

"I know. I was shaking a little myself," Kit agreed. "It
was just as well that Ned started to sneeze right then, or
I'm not sure that I could have maintained my usual hard-
headed masculine cool."

"That's okay. As I always say, there's only so much masculine cool a woman can stand."

"I don't recall you ever putting it that politely. Seriously,
though, sweetheart," Kit said, plucking a fragrant pink hibiscus blossom and slipping it behind his wife's ear. "Refresh my memory. When was it, exactly, that we decided
to invite the entire population of southern Florida to the
reception?"

"I'll give you a hint," Jilly teased, nestling herself
against his shoulder. Gently his hand stroked her hair.
"My head was lying on your chest, and your chest
was...sweaty."

"Ah. It all comes back to me. Remind me never to make
decisions right then. Afterglow is treacherous."

"Mmm. Our afterglow certainly is," Jilly murmured.
She turned her head to look in his eyes. "I love you, Kit."

"I love you, too, beautiful." Tenderly Kit kissed the tip
of her nose, the angle of her jaw, her flower-bedecked ear.
"I also love each and every one of our guests, in a different
way, of course," he said huskily, fingering the lace bow at
the nape of her neck. "But do you think that if I pulled the
fire alarm they'd all go home?"

"Nope. I suspect the Key West fire department would
just come over, and they're probably the only people in the
islands who aren't here already." Jilly lifted herself off
Kit's lap and stood in front of him. "However, I think that
if we were to carefully slide open the kitchen door, creep

very quietly up the back stairs and slip into one of the empty bedrooms, no one would even notice."

"Would Lavinia approve of us sneaking off to make love in the middle of her reopening reception?" Kit looked up at his wife, marveling at her beauty. In the warm yellow moonlight she looked like a goddess. A rather impish, mischievous and very sexy goddess. "It's not very proper behavior."

"She loathed proper behavior, remember? I bet she'd be disappointed if we didn't," Jilly said, reaching for her husband's hand.

Together, they looked back at the inn. It was noisy with talk and laughter and the babble of children. Sparkling with light, fragrance and color. Alive with generations of energy and life and love.

"You know, Jilly, sweetheart, I think you're right," Kit said, and they tiptoed silently indoors.

EVER HAD ONE OF THOSE DAYS?

TO DO:

☑ at the supermarket buying two dozen muffins that your son just remembered to tell you he needed for the school treat, you realize you left your wallet at home

☑ at work just as you're going into the big meeting, you discover your son took your presentation to school, and you have his hand-drawn superhero comic book

☑ your mother-in-law calls to say she's coming for a month-long visit

☑ finally at the end of a long and exasperating day, you escape from it all with an entertaining, humorous and always romantic Love & Laughter book!

ENJOY
Love & Laughter™
EVERY DAY!

For a preview, turn the page....

Here's a sneak peek at
Carrie Alexander's THE AMOROUS HEIRESS
Available September 1997...

"YOU'RE A VERY popular lady," Jed Kelley observed as Augustina closed the door on her suitors.

She waved a hand. "Just two of a dozen." Technically true since her grandmother had put her on the open market. "You're not afraid of a little competition, are you?"

"Competition?" He looked puzzled. "I thought the position was mine."

Augustina shook her head, smiling coyly. "You didn't think Grandmother was the final arbiter of the decision, did you? I say a trial period is in order." No matter that Jed Kelley had miraculously passed Grandmother's muster, Augustina felt the need for a little propriety. But, on the other hand, she could be married before the summer was out and be free as a bird, with the added bonus of a husband it wouldn't be all that difficult to learn to love.

She got up the courage to reach for his hand, and then just like that, she—Miss Gussy Gutless Fairchild—was holding Jed Kelley's hand. He looked down at their linked hands. "Of course, you don't really know what sort of work I can do, do you?"

A funny way to put it, she thought absently, cradling his callused hand between both of her own. "We can get to know each other, and then, if that works out..." she murmured. *Wow.* If she'd known what this arranged marriage thing was all about, she'd have been a supporter of Grandmother's campaign from the start!

"Are you a palm reader?" Jed asked gruffly. His voice was as raspy as sandpaper and it was rubbing her all the right ways, but the question flustered her. She dropped his hand.

"I'm sorry."

"No problem," he said, "as long as I'm hired."

"Hired!" she scoffed. "What a way of putting it!"

Jed folded his arms across his chest. "So we're back to the trial period."

"Yes." Augustina frowned and her gaze dropped to his work boots. Okay, so he wasn't as well off as the majority of her suitors, but really, did he think she was going to *pay* him to marry her?

"Fine, then." He flipped her a wave and, speechless, she watched him leave. She was trembling all over like a malaria victim in a snowstorm, shot with hot charges and cold shivers until her brain was numb. This couldn't be true. Fantasy men didn't happen to nice girls like her.

"Augustina?"

Her grandmother's voice intruded on Gussy's privacy. "Ahh. There you are. I see you met the new gardener?"

FORTUNE COOKIE

Breathtaking romance is predicted in your future with Harlequin's newest collection: Fortune Cookie.

Three of your favorite Harlequin authors, Janice Kaiser, Margaret St. George and M.J. Rodgers will regale you with the romantic adventures of three heroines who are promised fame, fortune, danger and intrigue when they crack open their fortune cookies on a fateful night at a Chinese restaurant.

Join in the adventure with your own personalized fortune, inserted in every book!

Don't miss this exciting new collection!

Available in September wherever Harlequin books are sold.

HARLEQUIN®

Let's Celebrate!

LOVE & LAUGHTER™

invites you to
the party of the season!

Grab your popcorn and be prepared to laugh as we celebrate with **LOVE & LAUGHTER**.

Harlequin's newest series is going Hollywood!

Let us make you laugh with three months of terrific books, authors and romance, plus a chance to win a FREE 15-copy video collection of the best romantic comedies ever made.

For more details look in the back pages of any Love & Laughter title, from July to September, at your favorite retail outlet.

Don't forget the popcorn!

Available wherever
Harlequin books are sold.

 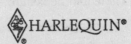 

HARLEQUIN WOMEN KNOW ROMANCE WHEN THEY SEE IT.

And they'll see it on **ROMANCE CLASSICS**, the new 24-hour TV channel devoted to romantic movies and original programs like the special **Romantically Speaking-Harlequin® Goes Prime Time.**

Romantically Speaking-Harlequin® Goes Prime Time introduces you to many of your favorite romance authors in a program developed exclusively for Harlequin® readers.

Watch for **Romantically Speaking-Harlequin® Goes Prime Time** beginning in the summer of 1997.

If you're not receiving ROMANCE CLASSICS, call your local cable operator or satellite provider and ask for it today!

ROMANCE CLASSICS

Escape to the network of your dreams.

As Seen on TV!

Free Gift Offer

With a Free Gift proof-of-purchase
from any Harlequin® book, you can receive
a beautiful cubic zirconia pendant.

This stunning marquise-shaped stone is a genuine cubic
zirconia—accented by an 18" gold tone necklace.
(Approximate retail value $19.95)

Send for yours today...
compliments of ◈ HARLEQUIN®

To receive your free gift, a cubic zirconia pendant, send us one original proof-of-purchase, photocopies not accepted, from the back of any Harlequin Romance®, Harlequin Presents®, Harlequin Temptation®, Harlequin Superromance®, Harlequin Intrigue®, Harlequin American Romance®, or Harlequin Historicals® title available at your favorite retail outlet, together with the Free Gift Certificate, plus a check or money order for $1.65 U.S./$2.15 CAN. (do not send cash) to cover postage and handling, payable to Harlequin Free Gift Offer. We will send you the specified gift. Allow 6 to 8 weeks for delivery. Offer good until December 31, 1997, or while quantities last. Offer valid in the U.S. and Canada only.

Free Gift Certificate

Name: _____

Address: _____

City: _____ State/Province: _____ Zip/Postal Code: _____

Mail this certificate, one proof-of-purchase and a check or money order for postage and handling to: HARLEQUIN FREE GIFT OFFER 1997. In the U.S.: 3010 Walden Avenue, P.O. Box 9071, Buffalo NY 14269-9057. In Canada: P.O. Box 604, Fort Erie, Ontario L2Z 5X3.

FREE GIFT OFFER   084-KEZ

ONE PROOF-OF-PURCHASE
To collect your fabulous FREE GIFT, a cubic zirconia pendant, you must include this
original proof-of-purchase for each gift with the properly completed Free Gift Certificate.

084-KEZR